Holiday Cream Cupcake & Murder (A Dana Sweet Cozy Mystery Book 5)

Ann S. Marie

Published by Ann S. Marie, 2017.

HOLIDAY CREAM CUPCAKE & MURDER

(A Dana Sweet Cozy Mystery, Book 5)

Copyright 2016 Ann S. Marie

All rights reserved; no part of this publication may be reproduced or transmitted by any means, electronic, mechanical, photocopying or otherwise, without the prior permission of the publisher.

This book is a work of fiction. The names, characters, places, and incidents are products of the writer's imagination or have been used fictitiously. Any resemblance to persons, living or dead is entirely coincidental.

This is a work of fiction. Similarities to real people, places, or events are entirely coincidental.

HOLIDAY CREAM CUPCAKE & MURDER (A DANA SWEET COZY MYSTERY BOOK 5)

First edition. February 1, 2017.

Copyright © 2017 Ann S. Marie.

ISBN: 979-8201268961

Written by Ann S. Marie.

Thanks to my Father above for every blessing.

HOLIDAY CREAM CUPCAKE & MURDER

(A DANA SWEET COZY MYSTERY, Book 5)

Murder strikes again in the small town of Berry Cove. Dana Sweet, part time mystery riddles blogger who has inherited the Cozy Cupcakes Café from her late grandmother, is once again drawn into a strange murder with a bizarre twist.

The Holiday spirit is in the air as the Mayor gets ready to host Berry Cove's Annual Christmas Banquet, but when the notorious town gossip columnist Shags Morefield is found dead holding a raspberry filled cupcake from the Cozy Cupcakes Café, all fingers point to Dana's cousin Katie who'd been the recent subject of her local gossip. Will Dana be able to figure out who's trying to frame her cousin in time?

A Dana Sweet Cozy Mystery series:
Strawberry Cream Cupcake & Murder (Book 1)
Blueberry Cream Cupcake & Murder (Book 2)
Chocolate Cream Cupcake & Murder (Book 3)
Strawberry Meringue Cupcake & Murder (Book 3.5)
Vanilla Cream Cupcake & Murder (Book 4)
Holiday Cream Cupcake & Murder (Book 5)
Valentine's Cream Cupcake & Murder (Book 6)
Buttercream Cupcake & Murder (Book 7)

Chapter 1

"AREN'T YOU EXCITED?" Katie asked her cousin Dana while piping the icing on a cupcake. She swirled the creamy frosting over the Holiday Cream Cupcake special of the week. The delicious frosting sent an aroma of ginger, mixed with cinnamon and vanilla that permeated the air.

Mmmm.

It made Dana's mouth water. It was already four o'clock in the morning, a few days before Christmas.

They had the satellite radio station set to Berry Cove's FM 99.9 where the DJ played holiday music for twenty-four hours around the clock. Right now, *Jingle Bells Rock* played and Dana felt all jingly inside for the first time in a long while since her ex-fiancé ran off with her roommate in New York and left her broken-hearted and broke, before she managed to pull her life back together.

Still, holiday cheer and the spirit of the season filled the mood in the town. Companies were more lenient with their staff and festively decorated and filled their offices with dessert treats—Dana should know since their café had gotten so busy they'd had to hire extra staff just to fill all the catering orders for some of the local businesses.

And this was Dana's first Christmas back in Berry Cove since she'd been a child, since moving back to the small town from New York, after her Grandma Rae passed away, leaving her the Cozy Cupcakes Café. Only, it hadn't been called that until Dana used her New York copywriting skills and changed the name of the café and a few things, to the chagrin of many naysayers in the beginning.

"Of course, I'm excited," Dana said, trying hard not to blush as she frosted the Gingerbread Cupcakes with fluffy cream cheese frosting piled high on the cupcake. Just the way Grandma Rae used to make them.

Dana used the same ingredients. For the cupcake she used: 5 tablespoons of unsalted, softened butter; half a cup of white sugar; half a cup of unsulfured molasses; one egg; one egg yolk; a teaspoon of ground cinnamon; one and a quarter teaspoons of ground ginger; one tablespoon of cocoa powder; half teaspoon of ground allspice; half teaspoon of ground nutmeg; quarter teaspoon of salt; one teaspoon of baking soda; half a cup of hot milk; quarter teaspoon of lemon extract; and one and a quarter cups of all-purpose flour.

For the Cream Cheese Frosting Dana used: two tablespoons of unsalted butter; two ounces of cream cheese; two third cups of sifted confectioners' sugar; and quarter teaspoon of lemon extract.

She had the oven preheated to 350 degrees Fahrenheit. She lined each batch of twelve cupcakes with cupcake liners. She creamed five tablespoons of the butter with the white sugar. Then she added the molasses and the egg and the egg yolk. She then sifted together the flour, cocoa powder, ginger, cinnamon, allspice, nutmeg and salt. Dana then dissolved the baking soda in the half a cup of hot milk. She added the flour mixture to the creamed mixture and stirred. She then stirred in the hot milk mixture and then poured the batter into the cupcake liners. She'd baked each batch for nineteen minutes.

HOLIDAY CREAM CUPCAKE & MURDER

For the frosting, she creamed the two tablespoons of butter and the cream cheese together, then she added the confectioners' sugar and beat it in until the mixture was nice and fluffy. She then added the lemon extract and beat the mixture. Only when the cupcakes were cool did she frost the tops.

Cozy Cupcakes Café decided to make two official Christmas cupcakes in addition to the many delicious cupcakes they served. One was the Gingerbread Cupcakes with cream cheese frosting and the other was the Christmas Cupcakes piled high with buttercream frosting decorated with colored sugar and filled with rich raspberry jam filling.

Right now, the café had a tall order to fill today since they were supplying the dessert treats for the Mayor's Christmas Party later this evening.

But that wasn't what had Dana's heart all giddy and fluttering inside her chest. A grin curved her lips at the thought of a special guy.

Drop dead gorgeous Detective Troy Anders.

The hot detective had finally asked Dana out on what looked like an official date. Her heart skipped a beat just thinking about it but she tried hard not to let it get to her head.

She never thought she'd ever go out on a date again after what her ex-fiancé did to her.

But then she thought to herself that Troy was probably just being congenial since she'd helped him out on a few of his murder cases recently—by chance, of course. She would just happen to be at the wrong place, right time and each murder involved one of the Cozy Cupcakes Café's cupcake of the day. She had to save her late Grandma Rae's café's reputation, of course. And being an online mystery riddles blogger only gave her more of an interest to figure out the real killers.

"Well, I sure hope that *woman* is not going to show up," Katie scolded, wrinkling her nose.

"That *woman*?" Dana queried. "Oh, wait a minute, I think I know whom you're referring to."

Mayor Headly Jones, Berry Cove's flamboyant mayor was hosting Berry Cove's Annual Christmas Party at the Town Hall.

All were invited, including the notorious Shags Morefield, the *Berry Cove Gazette's* new gossip columnist. Dana really couldn't believe the *Gazette* would even *hire* a gossip columnist. But in this day of internet popularity, the *Gazette* was trying to save itself from going under in the stiff competition by providing many intriguing new columns and inadvertently hired a former New York columnist, Shags, to join their team. She was only in town for a few months of the year before flying back to New York.

"Of course, she will be there. She's there every year, Katie," Inga, the baker, with her thick Russian accent said. Inga shoved another batch of cupcakes into the oven and closed the door. She then set the timer.

"Terry, can you get me another cupcake pan from the back," Inga said to one of the new temps.

Terry was a student at the university. A nice girl with brunette hair and thick black glasses on her very round face. She was very short and medium built. A pleasant addition to the café during the holiday season. If things worked out, Dana was thinking of hiring Terry permanently as a part time staff.

HOLIDAY CREAM CUPCAKE & MURDER

Dana liked being the boss. It was a change from her pencil-pushing job in the Big Apple. She had the authority to hire staff and make changes to the café as she saw fit. Though in the beginning when she first took over from Grandma Rae after her passing, she'd been met with hostility from everyone, since her grandmother was a favorite in the town and missed dearly.

"Sure thing," Terry said. She moved quickly to the back and returned with a pan and gave it to Inga. Terry had told Dana earlier that she hoped to open up her own café one day. Dana was all too glad to show her the ropes.

"Well, I don't want to see her," Katie continued her conversation with Dana.

"Oh, don't worry about her, cuz. I would just ignore her. Besides, most people around here know she's just full of steam. She'd be out of our hair soon."

"Don't count on it," Inga said as she whipped up the batter for another batch of cupcakes.

"What do you mean?" Dana asked puzzled.

"I mean, I heard from a girl who works at Bea's Salon that she's looking to move here permanently."

"Move here? Why?" Katie asked alarmed.

Katie really didn't like Shags. And for more than one reason. Katie had moved back to Berry Cove from New York after her failed divorce from her college sweetheart. That was years ago before Dana moved back. And guess who was at the heart of Katie's divorce?

Shags Morefield.

Shags had been the *other woman*, then ended up dumping Katie's ex-husband when she got what she wanted—meaning his money and moved on. Dana remembered consoling Katie after her divorce. And Shags had nothing but horrible things to say about poor Katie.

"I thought I got rid of that...woman when I moved back to Berry Cove," Katie pouted. "She makes my skin crawl."

"I know. I'm really sorry to hear that, too, Katie," Dana offered. Dana had been bitten by the "other woman" syndrome in her own relationship once before. And that bite still hurt at times. She could relate to the feeling of betrayal. "She has no right to want to move here."

"Yes, I know the type," Inga said while Terry, her assistant listened in with amusement, "She likes to taunt people. Especially the people she's hurt. And from what I hear, she's always hunting," Inga added.

"Hunting?"

"Yes, she's a hunter. Always digging for dirt, looking for gems of gold. She's got the goods on almost everyone you can think of. Always digging for dark family secrets, scandals, embarrassing lies..."

Dana shivered inside.

"That's awful," Dana commented. "Isn't it funny, that some people are blind to their own faults?" Dana said while swirling the last cupcake in her batch with freshly made whipped cream. Some touched her finger and she licked it off, the sweet vanilla mixture taste melted on her tongue.

"What do you mean?" Katie asked.

"I mean, Shags Morefield seems to have no conscious. *She's* the one that broke up *your* marriage by sleeping with your then husband and then she turns around and slams you in her column every chance she gets."

Katie had majored in theatre at NYU and had her first off Broadway show, when Shags—who happened to be a failed actress herself, didn't waste anytime in ripping all of Katie's performances to shreds. Shags' negative reviews were so harsh that it discouraged Katie and eventually she gave up on pursuing theatre—a bad mistake that Katie knew she would have to correct some day.

During Katie's early theatre days, her husband at the time had gone down to the newspaper office to have a word with the critic about tearing up his wife's earlier performances, but ended up falling for Shags instead. And of course, Shags continued to bash Katie in her reviews.

Katie eventually, after waiting tables and not getting anywhere, moved back to Berry Cove but she vowed one day to get back into the field. That was shortly after the divorce, of course.

"Tell me about it," Katie huffed. "I wish I could cancel her gossiping-mouth like I can cancel the subscription to her newspaper," Katie teased.

Dana grinned. "I'm sure it's just a rumor that she's moving to town."

"Oh, no it's not," Inga insisted, kneading more dough for their special Christmas bun. The crew was very busy this morning. So many tasty holiday treats to make before the café opened.

"Inga, you and I both know that as much as we love Bea's Salon to get our hair or our nails done, what you hear from the customers there may not necessarily be all true."

"But this bit of information is true. One of Bea's customers is a real estate agent."

"Rebecca?"

"Yes, that's the one. Rebecca said that Shags was looking to move here. She has enough money for a down payment. You know the prices of real estate in New York, right?"

"That's true," Dana said, almost to herself. She knew how costly it was to live there—never mind buy a house or condo apartment. It was out of reach for many people. But Berry Cove was another matter. House prices were heavenly there compared to major cities.

"Yes, well, she's looking at moving back here and I heard that she also has enough money to buy the Berry Cove Gazette."

"What? That's impossible."

"Oh, not really. She came into some money. So I heard."

"Probably blackmail money," Katie pouted.

"Oh, Katie. What's going on here, ladies? This is the holiday season. Tis the season to be *merry*, not *weary*," Dana said.

Dana didn't want to think about all that right now. And she knew why. "Remember what Grandma Rae used to say about your mood in the kitchen?"

"You're so right, cuz," Katie agreed. "Grandma Rae used to always say 'stay in a good *mood* when you're cooking *food*'," she grinned.

The girls both laughed with fondness over the memory. Grandma Rae was really a woman of words. That was why Dana came up with the idea to have the cupcakes piled high with whipped cream which could be eaten with a spoon and also included a cozy fun saying on the wrapper of the cupcake of the day to brighten a customer's day. It would be one of those

HOLIDAY CREAM CUPCAKE & MURDER 11

sayings Grandma Rae used to make up. Today's saying would be "Make the Holiday Cheer, Everywhere!"

Straight from Grandma Rae's wisdom to the customer. It was a way of keeping her spirit alive in the hearts of her beloved customers. Dana missed Grandma Rae like crazy, each and every day.

"Darn right, cuz," Dana added, "Grandma Rae would always tell us that your emotions can transfer to what you're cooking or preparing for consumption. It's like we channel our energy to our food or whatever we're doing. So we have to be mindful of what we're thinking and how we're feeling when cooking. Now who would want to consume angry food or food that was prepared when the chef was in a foul mood?"

"Not me, that's for sure." Katie laughed, wrinkling her nose.

"Exactly. Now, we're going to bake these delicious cupcakes for the Mayor's Christmas Party in a good mood and ignore any negativity out there. Besides, everyone in the town is counting on us. After all, why worry about something we can't change?"

"True." Katie and Inga said in unison.

Dana noticed that Terry the temp, didn't say much at all. Probably because she was new and shy and didn't want to get involved in office talk as a newbie.

"So, we're going to think positive going forward, yes?" Dana announced.

"Yes, we sure will," Katie agreed.

"Good." Dana got ready to shove another batch of cupcakes in the oven when she felt a chill slither down her spine. It was the raspberry jam filled cupcakes.

"You okay, cuz?" Katie said, noticing Dana's frozen expression.

"Um...I...I think so."

Oh, no. There was that feeling again. She looked at the tray of cupcakes. Oh, goodness no. She felt as if something bad was about to happen.

Chapter 2

DANA FOUGHT HARD TO shake off the feeling from earlier today at the café as she pulled out some dresses from her closet for her date with the hot detective Troy for the upcoming Mayor's Christmas Party later that evening.

She'd just had her bath and had her robe on, still trying to figure out what on earth she was going to wear tonight.

Truffles, her fuzzy little ginger haired cat lay cozy on the bed, watching her. "What should I wear, Truffs?" Dana asked as if Truffs could really respond.

Truffles looked on and purred gently.

Dana's heart melted. She felt a warm and cozy feeling center around her.

"You know, maybe I tend to over react at times. I mean, earlier today I felt a weird feeling with a batch of cupcakes I placed into the oven," Dana said as she held up a nice emerald green velvet dress to her while glancing in the mirror.

Dana had been very busy earlier today helping out in the kitchen. Even though they'd hired staff, the orders had been piling up with every small business in Berry Cove wanting catering for their office Christmas Parties, not to mention, the Mayor's office official party this evening. Though Dana often worked in the office, handling business affairs she was all too happy to help out with the baking today. Katie was still wrapping things up at the café and would be home soon to change for the party which would be starting soon at 6 p.m. It was already getting dark. It usually got dark around 5:30 p.m. at this time of the year.

"Maybe it was because we were discussing something we shouldn't have been. There's this woman moving into town, your auntie Katie's arch enemy. Katie really doesn't want her here. Actually, I don't think anyone wants her here but Grandma Rae is probably looking down on us and thinking that's not what the holiday spirit is about, right? We should be accepting, forgiving and using inclusion of others. So I think I'm going to change the way I feel and tell Katie the same thing…"

Truffles looked satisfied and purred.

"Okay, I cannot believe I am talking to my furry little cat," Dana whispered. "Okay, I need to get a life…"

Just then Dana heard the door open and close downstairs. "Katie!"

"Yep, it's me."

"Oh, good."

Dana heard Katie turn on the iPod downstairs and the song *All I want for Christmas is you* by Mariah Carey sounded magically through the speakers.

She heard Katie run up the wooden steps of the staircase.

"Hey, nice music," Dana commented while swaying to the beat of the festive classic. She had the dress in her hand twirling it.

"Thought it would be nice to get us all in the holiday spirit," Katie said.

"Cool." Dana paused for a moment and looked at her cousin. "Katie, have you been…drinking?"

"What me? No. I just had a little holiday cheer. Some of the guys from the suppliers came over and brought in some rum punch." Katie did a little dance.

"Katie. I'm so worried about you. You're not still worried about..."

"Nah, of course, not, cuz. I'm good, really. I...am...fine."

Dana could see hurt in Katie's eyes and felt sorry for her. Katie wasn't one to usually drink, not since her college days, but she was obviously bothered about the woman who ruined her life back in New York, now moving to her cozy hideaway home town of Berry Cove.

Katie's attention then turned to the bed where Dana had laid out several possible outfits. She'd already had her manicure and pedicure done yesterday at Bea's Salon. Katie had hers done the day before. They both sported red and green Christmas nail designs which looked spectacular. Dana was going to have a logo of the Café done but decided the holiday spirit designs would be best.

"Hey, fabulous," Katie said, picking up a little black dress.

"Oh, I don't think I'm going to wear that one."

"And why not, cuz?"

"I...um...I think it might send the wrong message. I'm going to wear the green velvet dress."

Katie wrinkled her nose.

"What wrong message? That you're beautiful and sexy and want to be with him?" Katie gave Dana a funny expression. "The green velvet dress," Katie said, holding the dress up with a funny look, "Looks like something Grandma Rae would wear. No. Forget it. Grandma Rae would *never* wear this if she was ever on a date."

"Katie."

"It's true. This old Victorian-looking frock, covers everything up and it looks frumpy on you. It's so heavy and shapeless."

Dana grinned. "No Katie. Besides, it's just a casual date."

"Now, which one of us is a little tipsy?"

"Katie!" Dana grinned.

"No, seriously, cuz. This hot detective guy *really* likes you. I know you've been too blind to see it because you've been hurt badly before, but don't go punishing yourself by never being attractive to anyone else."

Katie shoved the green velvet dress in the closet. "Remind me to burn that dress later. You are *never* wearing it. Ever. Where did you get it again, from a vintage rummage sale?"

Dana playfully rolled her eyes and shook her head. "No."

"Oh, it looks that way. Anyway, this little black number is perfect."

Katie held the dress up to Dana. "See."

The dress was hot. It was a curve-hugging long black dress with an open back. It looked sophisticated enough and yet sensual, too. Was Katie right? Her cousin always looked out for her. As she did for her cousin and all her family. One thing about the Sweet family was that they stuck together and looked out for one another, even though they might drive each other crazy from time to time.

"You know something, you're right, Katie," Dana said, holding the dress up to her and glancing in the mirror.

"I'm always right," Katie grinned. "Besides, isn't it Grandma Rae that always used to say, life is a dress rehearsal for eternity. Always look your best every day."

"Never be caught dead wearing something you'd regret, was what she used to say," Dana grinned.

Both girls laughed at the memory. It was as if Grandma Rae's spirit was always in the home, her words of wisdom and her humor would always be around them.

"Okay, time to get ready now."

"I KNOW I SAID IT EARLIER, but I have to say it again. You look...*beautiful*, Dana," Detective Troy said later at the party as the music played. His voice deep and silky and sexy.

Tingles erupted down Dana's spine. Her heart fluttered in her chest.

"S-so do you, Troy." And oh, boy did he ever.

He sported a sexy black tux with a black bow tie and filled out nicely in his suit with his broad muscular shoulders. He looked fit and gorgeous in his designer attire that had narrow notch lapels and a body-contouring cut. *Hot and sexy*. The scent of his sweet aftershave was intoxicating. Sensual.

His dark thick hair was slicked back and accentuated his high cheekbones and handsome facial features.

The mood was so festive at the party hall at the Mayor's Office in Town Square. The holiday lights flickered and glowed. The enormous Christmas Tree looked fabulous as it stood in the courtyard, lit with thousands of tiny flickering light bulbs. A light dusting of snow blanketed the city and the shop window panes. The scent of baked goods filled the air. The sound of Santa's bell ringing in the middle of the Town Square and the music from the carolers singing *Hark the Herald Angels Sing*, filled the air.

Who couldn't be in the Holiday Spirit now?

As they walked further into the enormous-red and green holiday decorated hall, Dana could see rows of tables with various treats lining them. Including a table with the Cozy Cupcakes Café's Christmas and Holiday baked goods. Trays of ginger cupcakes and raspberry filled cupcakes were laid out nicely.

"Hey, there, beautiful couple. Smile," Frank, the photographer from the Berry Cove Gazette said as he snapped their picture.

Beautiful couple?

Dana's spine tingled with delight at the words. Yes, they *did* look like a beautiful couple, didn't they? If only they *were* a couple.

Oh, what on earth was she thinking? It's only a one-time, date. He was a very busy detective and she was a very busy blogger and café owner. How on earth could they make this "coupling" work?

"Dana! Troy! You two look fabulous!" Bea, from Bea's Salon made her way over to them with open arms. "Look at you two," she continued.

"Thanks, Bea. You look fabulous yourself." She did. Bea wore dangling large red festive feather earrings and wore a beautiful red dress to match. She looked stunning.

"You look wonderful, Bea," Troy added.

"Why thank you both."

HOLIDAY CREAM CUPCAKE & MURDER   19

"Well, hello there, thank you so much for coming," Mayor Jones said as he approached them. "It's wonderful to see you here."

"Thank you, Mayor. We appreciate the invite," Dana said.

"Troy, is it possible to have a word with you privately?" the mayor asked, a worried expression on his face.

Troy looked concerned. "Sure. Dana, I'm really sorry, I'll be right back."

"No problem, Troy," Dana said, trying to hide the disappointment in her voice. She hoped everything was all right, but she was sorry to lose her date so soon.

After the men walked away, Bea inched closer to Dana.

"Well, it looks as if there's a new couple of the year, here," Bea winked. Bea's Salon was known as the gossip center of Berry Cove. Bea was a real sweetie and a good close and dear friend of Dana's late grandma, but Dana didn't know if she was ready to talk about a relationship that might not be.

"We're just good friends, Bea. Nothing more."

"Oh, really now?" Bea arched her brow. "Child, let me tell you something. That guy is hot and if you don't snatch him up soon, someone else will. Besides, you two look so great together. I see the way he looks at you when your back is turned. Girl, you've got one life to live. Live it. Stop working so hard around the clock that you can't get to enjoy life."

"You're right, Bea. But I'm serious. Nothing is going on between us. We're both busy in our careers."

Dana swallowed hard. The truth was, nobody wanted to be part of an "in" couple that ended up splitting apart. That would be the worst thing. She would rather date Troy quietly to see how things worked out. Besides, she'd had egg on her face before when her ex fiancé whom she'd doted about for years, ended up marrying her best friend instead. Her *ex*-best friend. It was a public humiliation she didn't want to go through again.

Katie then entered the party hall with her date, one of the suppliers for the café. But before Katie could move over to where Dana and Bea were, Gerdie Sue approached her first and they started chatting. The place was busy and filled with party guests already.

Waiters dressed in beautiful dark tuxes walked around the hall with trays serving guests treats and drinks.

"Here you go, ma'am," a waiter approached Dana and Bea. The tray had festive glasses filled with rich creamy eggnog drinks.

"Thank you," Dana said as she took a glass from the shiny silver tray.

Just then, the room seemed to go cold and the chatter hushed a bit. When Dana turned around, she saw who it was that walked in looking dangerous and sexy.

Shags Morefield.

The dagger eyes flew through the room. It was palpable.

Shags looked as if she didn't care. Shags walked in with her date, a hunky guy with sleeked back hair in a grey tux. He looked more like a bodyguard.

Shags did look stunning herself. She had a gold sparkly dress with her hair piled high on top her head and a gold tiara and other flashy jewelry. She'd always been eclectic from what Dana remembered.

Shags had apparently wanted to be an actress but failed. Was that why she became a critic and ended up cutting up

HOLIDAY CREAM CUPCAKE & MURDER 21

Katie's acting career? Now, of course, Shags had been promoted at the Gazette as gossip columnist.

Shags knew everyone eyed her with contempt, yet a wide smirk played on her face. It was more of a cocky look.

"Looks like the party died before it got started," Shags joked out loud.

Her companion chuckled.

What a sight.

A few of the guests approached Shags in a friendly manner in keeping with the holiday spirit. But from what Dana had heard, Shags had something on almost everybody. Something dirty. And if it wasn't dirty, sometimes, she'd make it up, Dana heard.

"Oh, boy, here comes trouble," Bea said, stroking her long red feathered earring nervously.

"Now, let's keep with the holiday spirit, Bea," Dana offered.

"You're right. It's just that no one wants her here. Not even the mayor."

"Not even the mayor? But why?"

"Because she'd blackmailed him before."

"Really? Then why would he invite her here?" Dana said with a glass of creamy eggnog in her hand. She took a sip and the rich vanilla drink soothed her throat. The taste of sprinkled nutmeg enhanced the drink. Each glass also contained a small stick of cinnamon. It was decorated so festively and creatively. Inga from the café really did a great job, Dana admitted. She'd been honored that Mayor Jones had asked her café to cater the dessert portion of the event.

"Because when the mayor sent the invite to the Gazette," Bea continued, "he had no idea *Shags* would come here too."

"Oh, right."

"You know he might be going through a divorce, right?"

"Yes, I heard."

"Well, I bet she's a factor in it. I heard that he had an affair with Shags."

"What? Are you sure?"

"That girl gets around. Her name ain't Shags for no reason."

"That's...awful. His poor wife."

"Exactly. My guess is that she threatened to tell his wife about their affair or she already did. Anyway, their marriage is in trouble. And I think the mayor is going to announce his retirement this year. He won't be running in the next election. Think he might even step down soon."

"Stepping down? Are you sure?" Dana was beyond puzzled.

She really liked Mayor Jones. Grandma Rae had loved him, too. He'd been an innovative thinker from the get go and he'd really turned the tourism industry around in a good way for the small town of Berry Cove. It would be a shame to see him leave office. He was in his early fifties and had so much energy.

Was that one of the reason's the mayor took Dana's date, Troy, away for a private word? Or was it about something else?

Dana's ever mystery-thinking mind was beginning to spin into overtime now. Thoughts swirled around in her head about the feeling she was having and how much almost everyone in the room wanted Shags to not be there.

Shags had shagged Katie's ex-husband, the mayor, and who knew who else?

Okay, positive thoughts, Dana. It's a holiday party. Where's the holiday spirit?

HOLIDAY CREAM CUPCAKE & MURDER 23

"I can't stand her myself," Bea continued.

Okay, there went the holiday spirit. Did anyone have anything nice to say about Shags Morefield?

"What do you mean, Bea?" Dana took another sip of eggnog.

"Oh, that girl is nothing but trouble. She...she tried to get me to give her some dough too. I tell you blackmail is her part time source of income. It's like she's some sort of spy or detective or something. I bet you she unscrupulously taps people's phones without them knowing it. I hear her ex used to work in the *spy business*."

"Oh?" Dana swallowed hard. Well, that wasn't good. Dana took another sip of her tasty eggnog. "Why would she want to get dough from you, Bea?"

Bea frowned for a moment. "Oh, its...never mind."

Oh, no. Did Shags find out an embarrassing secret about Bea?

Just then Shags sauntered over to where Bea and Dana were standing. Frank, the Gazette freelance photographer, who was making the rounds at the party was taking pictures of all the guests. He then approached them.

"Say cheese biscuits, ladies," Frank said with a wide smile.

The ladies all playfully rolled their eyes and grinned. They said cheese biscuit in unison and he snapped a few shots before thanking them and walking away to take more pictures of other guests.

"Hello ladies," Shags said, her jewelry dangling from her neck. She had massive earrings.

"Hello," Dana and Bea said in unison.

"Having a good time?"

"Yes, and you?" Dana said, trying to sound festive. She really didn't want to be a snob and besides, as Grandma Rae would say, "always be kind and courteous to people, regardless of what you hear about them, especially if they're being friendly to you. Being nice doesn't cost a thing," she would always say. Man, Dana missed Grandma Rae like crazy and wished she were still around.

Shags twirled her hair. "Oh, I'm very good thank you." She then turned to Bea. "Bea, you remember what we both spoke about earlier."

Bea seemed uncomfortable and shifted on the spot. That was so unlike her. There really must be something that Shags knew about Bea that Bea did not want anyone else to know.

"Um...yes. Yes, of course."

"Good. Don't forget. I'm heading back to New York on the weekend. I need to have it cleared before I leave." The woman smirked at Bea.

"F-fine. I'll see what I can do."

Bea nervously took a sip of her eggnog.

Dana narrowed her eyes at Bea and Shags. Just what was going on here?

Just then, a handsome young waiter approached them with a tray of delicious Holiday Cream Cupcakes. There were only five left on the tray. It looked as if the cupcakes had been going like hot cakes.

"Thank you," Bea said and took one of the cream filled cupcakes.

"Thanks," Dana said. She couldn't resist. Even though her café was catering, she always loved the taste of the treats. And why not? She was there as a guest tonight.

HOLIDAY CREAM CUPCAKE & MURDER 25

"Oh, no thanks," Shags said emphatically.

"You should try one, ma'am. They're really good," the waiter said as he offered Shags one.

"Oh, I heard about these killer cupcakes," she smirked. "I'll pass for now, thanks."

Shags then walked away.

Dana's heart fell.

She'd heard about these killer cupcakes? Who on earth did Shags think she was, dissing Dana's cakes like that?

"Oh, don't worry, child," Bea said, noticing Dana's frozen expression. "She always has something to say about everything."

"That's no help."

"Hello ladies, is everything all right here?" It was Sarah, Mayor Jones' loyal secretary.

"Yes, I'm fine thank you." After a round of insults from Shags Morefield, Dana was not going to let Shags ruin her evening. She would let those snarky comments about her killer cupcakes slide off her back like water off a ducks back.

"You sure?" Sarah said, her golden locks of hair dangling at her side in spiral curls. She wore a nice festive red holiday dinner dress and looked spectacular. So different than she usually looked when working at the mayor's office. She certainly dressed up for the occasion. It was so nice to see everyone sporting their finest attire and coming together to celebrate the holiday season. Dana noticed Sarah had a coat slung over her arm.

"I just saw Shags walked away, just making sure you're good," Sarah grinned. Everyone knew about Shag's snarky hostile behavior.

"Yes, she's quite a woman," Dana said.

Just then Bea excused herself and quietly walked away.

"Yes, she is," Sarah agreed. "I wouldn't worry about her."

"I can't believe the Gazette is giving her a full time job as a gossip columnist."

"Yes, it's true. But it's supposed to be some sort of parody column."

"Parody column?"

"Yes, almost like humor. I heard from the editor that she's going to do some sort of fictitious column to entertain readers with disguised news," Sarah said.

"Oh, I get it. She can't actually use real names because the newspaper could be libel," Dana said.

"Bingo. It's some sort of gimmick to help boost sales in this economic times with stiff competition from online entertainment. Everything seems to be about reality TV, YouTube and gaming. Subscriptions have been slipping apparently and the newspaper was thinking of closing down, but I guess Shags offered them some sort of deal based on her own popularity with that New York newspaper."

"Oh, right. I get it."

"Anyway, I'm just going to run out and get some more ice," Sarah said, putting her coat on, "See you later."

"Great. See you later."

Dana felt a bit self-conscious being there without her date. Was Troy still talking to the mayor? She scanned the hall and could see many faces of cheery guests being entertained, chatting with other guests, taking treats from the trays of waiters making the rounds, and drinking. But there was no sign of Troy, or Katie for that matter.

HOLIDAY CREAM CUPCAKE & MURDER 27

She frowned.

Then Dana sighed.

Not long after that everything went dark and there were a few screams.

"Not to worry, it looks as if we have a *blackout* guys," a voice called from across the room.

Oh, great. Where was Troy? Dana thought. She could really use him at her side right now. Dana stood still.

It was funny that the flood lights were not in operation. Everything was dark.

Just then, she spotted a waiter carrying a flashlight.

Then the emergency dim lights kicked in—albeit after a weird delay.

Some guests sighed heavily with relief. What a way to begin a holiday party. The sound speakers were quiet and all one could hear was the sound of murmurs and chattering amongst the guests.

Dana then walked over by the far corner where the dessert tables were to see if she could see Troy. She tripped and fell behind the table on something...

Or someone!

Dana let out a loud scream.

Just then Troy came out from the room behind the table. "Dana, are you all right?"

Troy followed Dana's horrified gaze as her eyes were fixed on what she'd stumbled on.

It was Shags Morefield. She had what looked like raspberry stains over her lips, a half-eaten cupcake by her head and she was turned on her side.

Troy leaned down and pressed his finger to Shags' carotid artery in her neck. He then shook his head and stood up.

"She's dead!"

Chapter 3

"SHE'S DEAD?!" DANA felt her heart explode in her chest. "B-but, how could that be? I...I just spoke with her ten minutes ago."

Dana's stomach felt queasy when she remembered the snarky comment Shags made about not wanting to eat any of the *killer* cupcakes.

But then it looked as if she'd eaten one of her cupcakes. And now she was dead!

Dana observed the body closely and noticed that Shags' gold tiara was missing, and...

Shags had what looked like a puncture wound in her back! There was a small circle of blood. But there was no knife around or sharp object that could have caused it. Not that Dana could see. Did Shags fall on something sharp when she...passed out? Or was she stabbed with a small sharp object first?

Dana gasped.

"Oh, no!" Dana covered her mouth with her hands. Troy leaned in and hugged her shoulders.

"It's all right, Dana." Troy then sighed heavily, his eyes filled with hurt.

Troy might be a cop, but Dana noticed that he always took his job seriously and despite what he did for a living, it tore him apart to see a murder victim. He'd told her that once. She really appreciated a guy who was tough on the job but one that also had a heart.

Troy then showed his badge to the rest of the guests who'd hovered around the area to see what was going on.

"It's okay, folks. I'm a detective. Nobody move, please." Troy then made a call for back up at the station to have his team there pronto.

This was a nightmare. Dana could not believe what was unfolding before her eyes. And good heavens! Another murder involving one of her Grandma Rae's famous cupcakes? Unbelievable!

Dana glanced around the room. Where were Bea, Katie and the mayor?

Who could have done this to Shags?

Then again, from what she'd heard from Bea, everybody could have a motive for wanting Shags Morefield silenced permanently. This was going to be a difficult case. Everybody also had a means and an opportunity. Especially during the black out!

Frank, the photographer, came out of the bathroom with his camera still in his hand.

Frank might have some clues caught on film.

Oh, Dana. What are you thinking? It was dark. No one might ever know who did it?

Shags might not have been the nicest person on the planet, but she sure did not deserve to be killed!

Dana went to the kitchen to grab an ice pack for her ankle that hurt after she'd tripped and fell over Shags' body. She placed the ice pack to her throbbing ankle. It looked as if it might have been twisted. She sat in the kitchen holding it to her leg, trying to imprison a sob from escaping her lips. She felt terrible about Shags. She felt terrible that her cupcake was at her lips. Or somebody had probably smeared it over her lips, trying to frame Dana's café once again. When she first moved back to the small town, not everyone was kind to her. She was like an outsider. They'd missed Grandma Rae. Those were tough shoes to fill. But now, she felt as if somebody had a lifelong vendetta to get her out of town. But she would not budge. She was going to stay there. No matter what. And she would carry on her grandmother's legacy. She wasn't going to frighten so easily.

"Hey cuz, you okay?" Katie's concerned voice sounded as she came into the kitchen.

"I'm fine as can be. Just a little shaken and stirred."

"Speaking of which. I could use a stiff drink myself," Katie murmured. "What happened to your ankle?"

"I tripped over Shags' body." Dana kept the ice pack pressed for fifteen seconds on then fifteen seconds off as she'd learned in First Aid.

"Oh, no. I'm really sorry she's...dead. But I didn't do it."

"Katie, I don't think for one moment you could be capable of...murdering Shags."

Dana then got up and went back out into the hall with Katie's assistance.

"Are you all right," Troy asked concerned as he held her arm.

"Oh, I'll be quite fine, Troy," Dana reassured.

Sirens sounded almost immediately.

Moments later, Troy left Dana's side to speak with the officers at the scene. They then sealed off the area where Shags' body lay.

A forensic photographer came to the scene.

"Looks like the victim passed out then fell on something sharp that punctured her back," the forensics guy commented.

"I see. Make sure you get all the angles," Troy said.

"Will do," he said.

So Dana's hunch was right. Shags must have fallen on a sharp pointed object.

Oh, no.

Just then a flash went off in Dana's mind. *Frank!* Frank the Gazette freelance photographer. He must have seen something. He'd been busy taking snapshots of everyone all evening.

She would speak to Frank soon to ask him if he'd taken pictures of the area where Shags' body lay. No, wait a minute, the last thing she wanted to do was step on Troy's investigative toes. She would ask Troy to ask Frank about his photos on his camera.

There must be some clues there. Was the cupcake poisoned? Was that why she passed out? Dana's stomach twisted into knots thinking that one of her cupcakes was again at the center of a crime. But she also wanted to know who stood near the dessert table moments *before* Shags was murdered.

Dana felt her stomach tighten when a forensic scientist carefully picked up the cupcake by Shags' side and placed it in a clear evidence bag.

"Oh, great. Another cupcake off to the lab." Her cupcakes must have seen the inside of more police labs than a criminal's DNA on an episode of CSI.

Dana really felt that her cupcakes were not the cause this time. She just felt it deep in her soul. Everyone knew about the last few murders that happened to have cupcakes from the Cozy Cupcakes Café on the scene either eaten by the victim or near to the victim. Besides, in this case, there was a stab wound on the victim's back. Maybe Shags didn't fall on something sharp. Maybe she was stabbed first?

Dana gasped again. She saw a long red long-feathered earring near the table, near the body.

Oh, no. Bea wore that earring. Her heart raced in her chest.

She remembered Bea saying that she had to speak to Shags later about some payment. Did they meet? Did they have a disagreement?

Either way, Dana had to speak to Troy. And fast, before the murderer splits the scene.

A chill slithered down her spine. No matter which way she sliced this cake, there was a murderer amongst them—right this moment. And he or she could strike again.

Chapter 4

"TROY, YOU NEED TO GET hold of Frank, the photographer," Dana said moments later after Troy had interrogated a few of the guests. Shags's body had already been hauled off to the coroner's office.

"I'll be getting to him soon, Dana."

"No, Troy. You don't understand. You need to do it now."

"Why is that? Dana, do you know something?"

"He must have seen someone. The culprit. Somebody must have been near to Shags over by the dessert table."

"Sam," Troy said, turning to one of his men, a uniformed cop. "Get Frank over here with his camera, stat."

"Sure thing, boss," Sam said.

"Thank you," Dana breathed a sigh of relief.

"I'll interview him next and see what we can get from those images, but I still don't think any of what he has on his camera will help at this point."

"But you're not seeing it from my perspective."

"Which is?"

"Whomever was near Shags just before the blackout could have done it. They had the *means*."

He frowned. "Dana. We can't just go by means. We'll need a strong motive."

Dana furrowed her brows. "Troy, can I speak with you privately, please."

"Sure."

HOLIDAY CREAM CUPCAKE & MURDER   35

They walked away from any potential prying eyes or ears over to a far corner of the hall where no one could hear them.

"What's wrong, Dana?"

"You mean besides the obvious?" Dana arched the brow. "There's been a horrible murder and I feel that someone's trying to pin this on one of the cupcakes from the Cozy Cupcakes Café."

"Dana."

"Troy." She placed her hands on her hips. "Before you say it. I'm not paranoid. It seems like such a copy cat case of what happened before with that Gazette reporter who slammed my Grandma Rae's café after I took it over."

"I remember that case all too well, Dana."

"Now, another reporter from the Gazette, the newest columnist who writes gossip, is found dead with a cupcake at her mouth. Doesn't that seem a bit...odd? Coincidental?"

"All right. You do have a point." Troy took out his notepad and began making some notes. "Go on."

"Well, first of all, Shags was offered a cupcake when the waiter made his rounds."

"And?"

Dana swallowed hard. "W-well, she told him she would pass for now because she'd heard about...the...killer cupcakes."

"I see," Troy said, scribbling down some notes.

Oh, no. What had Dana just said? The truth.

Tell the truth Dana. Don't hold back from Troy. He needs to know everything. Even at the risk that she'd sound crazy.

"I just had no idea that when she said she would *pass* for now...that she would end up *passing* away soon after." Dana gulped. The tragic irony was unbelievable.

"But then she changed her mind, didn't she?"

"What do you mean?" Dana asked.

"She did end up eating one of your cupcakes."

"Troy," Dana said, leaning in closer to him, her voice a whisper. "I think that's what the killer wants us to believe."

Troy ran his fingers through his dark sexy mane of hair. "Why would he or she do that, Dana?"

"Because Troy, there were so many guests around us at the time. And they'd heard what she said. What if one of them poisoned the cupcake ahead of time."

"Sam," Troy said, "make sure none of the waiters leave the scene."

"Yes, boss. Billy's questioning them now."

"Good."

Dana's heart skipped a beat. Did someone slip a cupcake on one of the waiter's tray and tell him to give one to Shags?

Her mystery riddles thinking mind was working overtime now.

Sam then approached Troy and Dana. "Think you might have something there, boss."

"What is it, Sam?"

"One of waiters said that someone told him to offer the cupcake to Shags."

"Oh, really now?"

"Yes, sir."

"And who was that?"

"He gave us a description. It was a woman dressed in a blue velvet dress."

"Is she here?"

HOLIDAY CREAM CUPCAKE & MURDER 37

"It's possible that she left, sir. But we found a red feathered earring by the victim's body."

Dana had to say something. "Troy, I think I know who that belongs to but I really don't think it had anything to do with the case."

"Who's is it?"

Dana swallowed hard. She turned around and saw Bea approaching them with one earring in her ears. "It's mine, detective. That earring's mine but I did not kill Shags."

"I see," Troy said. "Please don't go anywhere Bea. We need to speak with you."

"Fine, Detective. I did have a meeting with Shags and we kind of got into a heated argument. But...I didn't do it. I...I swear to you."

Dana sighed, feeling sorry for Bea.

"Sam will take your statement, Bea. And Sam have our men get on the case of the woman in the blue velvet dress. Thanks."

Sam left them alone.

Troy then turned his attention to Dana, an appreciate glance in his eyes. "I owe you one, as usual, Dana. Good thinking."

"I just hope we find the killer in time, Troy. And...Troy," Dana hesitated for a moment.

"Yes, Dana."

"Where *is* the mayor?"

Just then, Sarah, the mayor's secretary came rushing into the party room. "Oh, no. What happened?"

"Shags is...dead," Dana sputtered.

"What? How?" Sarah looked alarmed. "Where's the mayor?"

"He's speaking with one of our officers," another cop said.

Sarah had a bag filled with ice. Dana then remembered that she'd gone to get ice earlier.

"I need to speak to him," Sarah said, "I just need to put these in the kitchen first."

Sarah then hurried off toward the kitchen.

"Troy, we need to get hold of the security tapes here. I need to see who left and who entered."

"Our men are already on it."

"Is it possible to see the footage with you, Troy?"

"Dana that's not standard procedure."

"But Troy if one of my cupcakes was on the scene, I have a right to know why. Besides, I might be able to find some clues. You yourself said once that I have an unusual eye for picking up on fine details."

"Fine, since you put it that way," he said, arching a brow. He looked positively adorable whenever he did that.

She just hoped she would find the killer soon, or else.

Chapter 5

LATER, DANA SAT BESIDE Troy in the security room with the security team. She didn't want to say anything and for the first time that evening, she felt intimidated.

Troy's eyes were fixated on the monitor as he watched each screen and what each guest was doing at the time.

They watched a shot of the photographer Frank walking around, looking at everyone then taking snapshots.

There was a scene with Dana walking in with Troy. Her cheeks felt hot when she saw how good they looked together on camera. They looked more like an A-list celebrity couple than a hot detective and local baker. Still, Troy looked deliciously handsome in his tailor-fitted tux which accentuated his broad shoulders and his tall physique.

Dana then noticed a woman with long blond hair in a black curve hugging dress and carrying a black designer bag over her shoulder. The flap of the bag was noticeably opened. She approached one of the waiters. The woman started to make conversation with the waiter.

Then she walked away. Their backs were turned to the security camera so it was hard to say what happened next.

"Do you think that's the woman who told the waiter to give the cupcake to Shags?"

"The waiter said she was wearing a blue dress, didn't he?"

Dana felt deflated. "That's true."

Then she remembered the fact that eye-witness testimony was not always reliable. People tended to remember things differently. Maybe it *was* the woman.

There was a surveillance clip of Bea meeting with Shags by the dessert table. The ladies got into a heated argument and Bea's earring fell off without her noticing it, apparently. Then Bea gave Shags an envelope and looked around to see if anyone was watching. She then walked away.

"Make note of that," Troy said to the security. "I'm going to need that clip."

"Sure thing," the security officer said.

Then there was another scene with the mayor at the scene, looking around suspiciously in the crowd. He then spotted Troy and Dana and continued to look around. He then asked to speak with Troy and they both left.

Dana swallowed hard. She remembered that all too well. The mayor stole her date for most of the evening.

The security officer then showed another clip.

"Zoom in over there," Troy said to the security personnel.

"Sure thing," the security personnel said before enhancing a shot.

"Isn't that your cousin, Katie?" Troy asked.

"Yes, it is." In the footage, Katie approached one of the waiters, the same waiter from the other clip, and seemed visibly upset about something. What on earth were they talking about?

Then there was another surveillance clip showing Katie walking over to the dessert table and glancing over the cupcakes tray. Shags then approached her from behind. Katie spun around. She seemed to have a few choice words for Shags.

Both women got into a heated argument. Then...the lights went out. Blackout.

"I think we've found our killer." Troy's voice was stern.

"Found your killer? Who?"

"Your cousin, Katie."

Dana froze.

Chapter 6

"KATIE? THE KILLER? No way, Troy!" Dana protested.

"Dana!"

"Troy!"

"Guys, let's get her in for questioning." Troy then turned to his men who were also in the room observing the security tapes.

Dana felt her stomach squeeze. Her heartbeat pounded in her chest. There was no way Katie could have done it. No way.

"But why would she?"

"We spoke to one of your temps from the bakery earlier. She's here now. She'd told us that Katie had made a threatening statement at the café."

"Terry?"

Dana's mind reeled back to earlier that morning in the kitchen. Terry had been listening attentively to their conversation though not adding anything of her own when Katie went on about how much she couldn't stand Shags and wished she could…cancel Shags like she canceled the subscription to her newspaper.

Oh, good heavens.

Of course, Grandma Rae's words came back to her: "Remember to keep your words soft and sweet, because tomorrow you might have to eat them."

It looked as if Katie might have to eat her own words now, God forbid. Katie was only blowing off steam when she spoke about Shags earlier.

"Your cousin Katie had the motive," Troy said. "She had the means and opportunity. The video surveillance tapes proves it, Dana." Troy's eyes looked sad. He really didn't want to do this but it was his job. What could Dana say? Her own cousin who helped her managed the Cozy Cupcakes Café was going to be arrested for murder and there was nothing she could do about it, except...

"Troy, did you find the source of the power outage?"

"The what?"

"The source?" Oh, boy. There went Dana Sweet's overactive mystery-riddles mind. "If you ask me, Troy. It seems very convenient that Shags shows up here. Nobody wanted her here in town. Let's face it, the holiday spirit in the hall got a bit of a chill when she came waltzing in with her date for the evening. And it seemed so coincidental that while she was near the dessert table, the lights went out. She was killed."

Troy thought for a moment. "You do have a point, Dana. But for now, we still need to take your cousin in for questioning."

Dana frowned.

This holiday evening was not going as planned. It was supposed to be ' tis the season for *giving*,' not *killing*!

Oh, yoy, yoy!

Chapter 7

"WE FOUND OUT THE SOURCE of the outage, sir," Officer Sam said to Troy as he walked into Troy's office at the precinct later that evening.

"What happened?"

"It was the entire block that was knocked out of power for that time period."

"The entire block?"

"Yeah, that darn utility box at the end of the street. It's near a tall tree. Whenever there's a snow storm, it always gets knocked out. It looks like a vehicle hit it."

"Well, how *convenient* for the killer," Dana commented as she sat in Detective Troy's office.

"Yes, it *is* very convenient," Detective Troy agreed.

Katie was being questioned in the next room by another detective on the case as a person of interest. Imagine that? Katie. A person of interest in a murder investigation? Dana swallowed hard and tried to keep her heartbeat from smashing against her rib cage.

Keep calm, Dana. There's no way they would arrest Katie for the murder of Shags.

At least she hoped they wouldn't arrest her.

Aunt Nia and Uncle Merv were on their way down to the station to see Katie.

Troy had been so nice to Dana and offered her the opportunity to wait in his office while her cousin was being interrogated, knowing how difficult it was for Dana to have her own family member under suspicion. He probably also felt a bit guilty for abandoning his date for the evening, too. It was turning out to be some date. A date with crime more like it.

"Oh, Katie, are you all right?" Dana rushed to Katie's side as she came into Troy's office looking visibly shaken.

What on earth did they do to Katie?

"I...I'm fine, cuz. Just a little shaken up."

"What?"

"Oh, no. It's not that, they were nice to me. I just...it's just so much happening this evening."

"I understand."

"Ma'am," the officer who walked in with Katie said, "We're going to ask that you not go anywhere and to surrender your passport."

Katie looked as deflated as Dana felt.

"Yes. Of course."

"It's standard procedure, Katie," Troy said.

"I know," Katie said, quietly.

"I'm so glad you're not under arrest," Dana said.

"You and me, both, cuz."

They were probably gathering more evidence to use against Katie. Dana was going to have to act fast if she wanted to spare her cousin. She remembered Katie was claustrophobic. She couldn't handle being in a small closed off enclosure for too long. Katie couldn't even last in an office cubicle at a regular job. That was why she always tried to get into showbiz. She had to work in wide open spaces.

Speaking of wide open spaces. Dana just thought of something.

"WHERE ARE WE GOING?" Katie asked Dana as they hurried back to the car after leaving the police station.

"Back to the scene of the crime, cuz."

"Hey, no way, hosay. I've had enough of that creepy place." Katie hugged herself in her winter coat and pink scarf and matching hat.

The snow flakes fell softly on the town as the wind gently blew a light dusting of snow. It wasn't too cold. Just right.

"Katie, you don't understand. I think we're missing something. Don't you want to find out who really killed Shags?"

"Of course I do."

"Well, we're going to have to do a little observation of our own if we want to make sure the cops don't miss anything. The last thing you want is to be pinned down for a crime you didn't commit."

"But there'll be caution tape around the area."

"I left some of our trays there. We have a reason to go back to the Town Hall."

"True."

"Besides," Dana said starting up the car, "look around you, cuz. What do you see?"

"Katie sat in the passenger side and looked around outside. "I see two young chicks siting in a car outside the police station waiting to do something really stupid. What do you see, cuz?"

"Very funny, Katie," Dana grinned. "Look at the ground outside."

"Yes. It's snowing."

"It's snowing now, but it wasn't snowing earlier."

"What's your point, cuz?"

"My point is the snow flakes are literally melting on the ground now."

"And?"

"And I'm curious to find out how on earth, during a perfectly nice evening where the roads are clear that a truck, car or van or whatever it was, rammed into a utility box to knock out power in the area of the Town Hall."

"Oh. I never thought about that."

"Precisely. I recall the last time something like that happened it was during a terrible storm and the driver of the vehicle lost control and slammed into the utility box. There was zero visibility *then* and the roads were slick and slippery. Not the case right now, of course." Dana pulled out of the parking lot and drove up Maple Street toward the Town Hall.

"I see the wheels spinning in that mystery-solving head of yours, cuz. What are you thinking?" Katie interjected Dana's thoughts.

"There's something that's a bit off, Katie. Something is bothering me. Something is just not adding up here. And I am dying to find out what it is."

Chapter 8

A FEW BLOCKS FROM THE Town Hall, Dana stopped the car. She then grabbed her coat from the back seat and got out at Maple Street.

"Dana, are you sure you know what you're doing?" Katie seemed concerned and anxious.

"I sure hope so."

Dana then made her way to the trunk of the car and popped open the door. She then searched around and grabbed her flashlight.

She walked carefully to the side of the road and over to the dented utility box that was knocked over. The wind blew her hair in her face. A sudden chill came over her. She knew she had to be crazy. What on earth was she doing there? What was she looking for? What was she hoping to really accomplish there? If Detective Troy ever found out she was snooping around that area, he would have a coronary. But she had to do something. Her cousin's life was at stake. So was her café. So was the town's safety if a cold-blooded killer was still on the loose.

"Do you see anything?" Katie asked, coming out of the car.

"Not yet," Dana said as she walked over to the utility box. It was difficult to see clearly in the night. But she was looking for some sort of clue. The utility box looked more like aluminum and had a dark green tint to it and some mud on the bottom. It was about five or six feet in height and a few feet in width from what Dana could guess.

HOLIDAY CREAM CUPCAKE & MURDER

"Just to think, there are thousands of tiny high voltage wires running through that thing. The city should have it more hidden from view off the roadside."

"You would think."

"So many addresses are connected to this box. All it takes is for just one blow and power would be knocked out to hundreds of addresses," Dana thought out loud.

"Creepy, isn't it?"

"Tell me about it."

"But Dana, it was an accident. It had to be."

Dana frowned. Just then she pulled out her cell phone. "Here, hold this flashlight to that area there. I'm going to take a snap shot."

Katie held the flash light pointed to the broken box. Dana then took a few pictures with her cell phone camera. When she looked back at the images, the snapshots were a bit grainy considering the night and the weather.

"Doesn't that look like white paint?"

Katie looked closer at the image that Dana zoomed up on her screen. "It sure does. But it could have been there for a while."

"I don't know. I hope Troy is planning on looking for a white-colored vehicle with possible paint damage to the front."

Just then the girls heard a loose tree branch snap on the ground in the wooded area by the utility box.

"Who's there?" Katie pointed the flashlight.

There was a tall man with broad shoulders moving toward them in the dark.

Dana gasped.

"You two ladies all right?" the deep voice sounded as he came into the view of the street lamp.

Dana breathed a sigh of relief. "Mayor Jones. I...I'm surprised to see you here," Dana said, incredulously.

The mayor was sporting his thick winter three-quarter length wool coat and had black leather gloves on and his leather black cap. A tweed scarf was wrapped around his neck to keep him warm.

"I was...um...just taking a walk. I heard the area was knocked out of power because of the utility box again."

Dana glanced around. "Looks like the Berry Cove Utilities Department got to work right away, eh?" The street lamps were lit and a few of the homes down the street had power.

"Yes, we've managed to restore power to many of the homes that was knocked out, including the Town Hall, of course. I'm still going to be working on it to make sure everyone gets power restored." He clasped his hands together.

Dana noticed there was a slight tear on his leather glove. Mayor Jones was always impeccable with his dressing. There was usually never a crease on his ironed clothes. But the gloves he wore looked worn and torn.

"Good," Dana said, her breath making a white puff in the cool evening air.

"I...um...I guess, I should be running now," Mayor Jones voice was quivering and cool. Perhaps he was cold. Or was he nervous? Dana couldn't quite tell right now. But something was sure off.

"I just wanted to see how much damage was done here," Mayor Jones continued. "I'm thinking of having this thing covered in the future. It's the second time power has been knocked out to the block in the space of a year. Maybe the box is in a bad location."

"Or maybe there needs to be some sort of barrier to prevent this from happening again."

"Good call, Dana. Have a good evening, ladies."

That was their cue to leave, too.

"You too, Mayor. Oh, and I'm so sorry about what happened to poor Shags. What an awful thing to happen to her and at the Town Hall party, too."

He looked away then looked down at his feet. "Yes, it was a terrible thing."

❦

"WELL, THAT WAS ODD," Dana said as she started up the car.

"What was odd?"

"The fact that the mayor came out late at night *by himself* to look at the damage done to the utility box. If I didn't know any better I would swear he was up to something or up to covering something up. *And* do you realize that he never once questioned why *we* were there."

"Yes, that is true. Was it because he's guilty of something? Do you think?"

"I do, cuz. I really do. He's definitely hiding something. I wish I knew what it is. And secondly, when I made the comment about Shags being murdered he agreed that it was terrible."

"It *was* terrible. What's wrong with what he said?"

"It's what he *didn't* say after it that bothers me."

"Dana, what are you getting at, cuz?"

"I thought he would have said, yes it's terrible that Shags was murdered and yes, we're going to *catch* who did it?"

Katie gulped. "Do you think he did it?"

Dana looked at Katie then fixed her eyes back to the road as they made their way down to the Town Hall.

"I don't know, cuz. I really don't know—yet."

Chapter 9

"THE GOOD THING ABOUT the mayor being at the scene of the broken utility box is that he's *not* at the Town Hall."

"Dana, what are you up to?"

"Oh, nothing. Maybe we can go poking around his office."

"Are you crazy?"

"That really depends," Dana grinned.

Katie playfully rolled her eyes. "Dana, you know what I mean. He's the *mayor*! Besides, he'll be back soon."

As they pulled up to the Town Hall, Dana looked around. "Do you notice something, cuz?"

"No. What?"

"There's power everywhere. Everywhere is lit up right now."

"That's good, isn't it? Yes, but why did the mayor say that he's working to restore power to the rest of the homes and businesses in the area. The utility box on Maple covers this very block!"

Katie looked stunned. "It's true. It does."

Dana pinched her lips together.

"It looks as if a lot of people had reason to want Shags dead, but we need to find the one with the strongest motive and the best opportunity and the means." Dana sighed.

"Sorry, ma'am, you can't go back there," a security guard said to them as they tried to enter the building.

"Oh, I'm Dana Sweet from the Cozy Cupcakes Café. We were here earlier. We're just here to pick up our serving trays."

"Sorry, ma'am it's a crime scene. Police has asked that no one come in or out for tonight."

Dana frowned. "Very well. Thank you."

Dana felt deflated. She was willing to bet the Mayor, the big boss, was allowed back there as he wished. Perhaps then he would destroy any incriminating evidence.

Dana then had a thought as she walked back to the car. "You know cuz, we should probably look around at the back."

"For what?" Katie said, shivering in her coat.

"Katie, you're cold. Why are you wearing that thin coat?"

"This is a very nice coat."

"But just because it *looks* nice doesn't mean it does the trick."

"You mean I should wear a big fat puffy coat that makes me look ten pounds heavier?" Katie grinned and arched her brow as she glanced at Dana's massive puffy coat.

Dana smiled. "Like the one I'm wearing?" she arched a brow. "Good thing, I saw that you were tossing it out into the GoodWill bin or..." Dana froze. "That's it!"

"What's it?"

"The bin. Let's go check out the bins out back."

"Oh, no, cuz. You can't go searching through the garbage. I'm going to call it a night. I've had enough of being stuck in dirty crammed places for the night."

"Oh, cuz. Of course, how awful for you to be taking into the station like that. No worries. Just stay here and keep watch."

"Dana. I hope you know what you're doing."

"I do. I think."

Katie playfully rolled her eyes. "Oh, boy. Here we go again."

Just then Dana looked around and saw a large bin and opened it. She flashed her flashlight into the bin. "I think I'm going to have to get a nose clip, Katie. It does *not* smell very Christmassy in here."

"That's because it's the garbage bin, cuz. Do you really have to do that?"

"Katie, you know the rules of solving a crime. The first thing people want to do is get rid of evidence fast. What other way would they be able to do that?"

Dana climbed on top of a rock to peek in further. "I think I see something. Some ripped shreds of paper with handwriting on it. Holy crap! I think we're on to something, cuz."

"What do you see?" Katie asked, shivering and rubbing her arms while waiting by the car as a lookout.

"I see tons of torn paper. That's weird."

Dana then took a deep breath. "I'm going in for the dive. Wish me luck." Dana climbed inside the bin to see if she could pull out the torn letters.

Just then the back door of the building opened.

"Dana!" Katie tried to warn Dana.

It was too late.

Chapter 10

DANA FELT A TON OF garbage pour over her while she was in the bin. She thought she would drown in leftover desserts and food.

"Oh. My. God." Dana heard Katie shriek.

"Oh, no. This is awful." Dana felt wet and slimy as torn bags of garbage had been tossed into the bin with her inside it. She tried not to inhale for fear of gagging.

She heard the click clacking sound of heels on the pavement coming closer to where she was.

"Are you all right?" Katie shouted.

"I've had better days," she replied, feeling rather foolish and trying not to panic.

Dana managed to stand up in the large bin and shoved the papers she'd found in the bin into her pocket.

She then proceeded to climb out of the bin. Scraping her heels on the side, mounting on a pile of garbage bags to give her a boost.

"Oh. You look awful, cuz!" Katie said as Dana climbed out.

"Thanks, Katie."

"I sure hope it was worth it going in there."

"I think I may have…"

Just then, blue and red lights flashed as a police siren sounded.

"Oh, no." Could this night get any worse?

HOLIDAY CREAM CUPCAKE & MURDER 57

Dana had her leg hanging over the garbage bin, her black velvet high heeled shoe dangling. And her stocking slightly torn was in full view up to her thigh.

What a sight she must be.

Just then Troy came out of one of the cars.

Yep. This night is getting worse.

Now, she was really in trouble.

"Dana! What are you doing there? Are you all right?" Troy's voice sounded more alarmed and concerned than annoyed. Okay, that had to be a good thing, right?

"Um...oh, Troy. I was...um...looking for something." Okay, that wasn't exactly a lie now, was it? She was looking for something. She just wasn't going to bother him with little details right now until she was sure. Little details as in she was looking for evidence against the mayor—his boss.

Dana realized from speaking with Troy earlier that it would be like walking on thin ice to insinuate that the good old mayor of Berry Cove could possibly have something to do with a horrible crime like murder in his own territory—at the Town Hall. So Dana had to be sure first before she went rattling any holiday feathers.

"In the garbage, Dana? You lost something in the garbage bin?" He stretched out his hand to help her down and before long his strong arm was around her waist as he carefully lifted her down on to the ground from the bin.

He didn't even seem phased or bothered that she'd been covered in garbage. She felt a surge of heat and warmth around her as Detective Troy held her for that moment.

"I guess you're pretty turned off me now, huh? Being covered in...garbage."

"No, Dana. There's nothing in the world that would turn me off you." His voice was low.

"Not even being covered in trash?"

"Not even. Nothing can dampen your beauty."

Dana's heart fluttered in her chest. Butterflies tickled her tummy.

Nothing could dampen my beauty? Oh, my God. He did not just say that. Well, isn't that just...so...sweet.

Boy, did *he* really know how to make a woman covered in garbage feel good. Her ex-fiancé, a hot shot Manhattan advertising executive, had once seen her late at night at the office pulling a late shift. Her hair was frazzled and her make-up was worn and he'd actually had the nerve to say that she looked like crap and she should check herself in the mirror before he kissed her. Imagine that. Well, that should have been the first sign that he was not the one for her. But Troy was different, wasn't he? He was a true gentleman.

For that one instant, it was as if they were the only two at the back of the building. She'd almost forgotten that Katie was there and a couple of cops, who were now searching around the area looking for something.

She glanced into his beautiful blue eyes that seemed to sparkle under the moon light. The dim light from the street lamp above and the soft sprinkling of snow flakes seem to heighten his good features, his strong jaw line and his lovely eyes and shapely lips.

He still held her in his arms. It was as if he was Superman and she was Lois Lane from the original *Superman* movie where Superman caught Lois from a helicopter that was hinged on a building. The wind blew in Detective Troy's dark hair.

HOLIDAY CREAM CUPCAKE & MURDER 59

Her nostrils caught the sweet scent of his cologne or was that aftershave? Either way, he smelled delicious. Which was more than she could say for herself right now.

"You okay?" he said, interrupting her daydream.

She broke out of her trans immediately and nodded slowly. "Um. Yes. I...I'm fine. Now."

He then placed her down on the ground. "What were you really doing in there, Dana?" He arched a brow. His voice was filled with concern.

"Um, Dana, I think I found my earring," Katie chimed in to Dana's surprise.

"Your earring?"

"Yes, here it is." Katie dangled her earring in the air. "Grandma Rae gave it to me when I moved back here. It's a precious family heirloom."

Detective Troy didn't seem too convinced just then. "Very well, Katie, Dana. Please stay away from this area. It is a crime scene. I don't want to see either of you get hurt. I'm serious."

"I know." Dana felt her heart go kaboom in her chest. She knew how much Detective Troy was concerned about their safety. And she had no intention of being a stiff especially around the holiday season.

"We'll be very careful," Dana confirmed.

"Yes, we will," Katie agreed, shivering. She then motioned to Dana that she would be heading back to the car where it was warmer than outside. Dana knew Katie had the keys and would turn on the ignition.

"Good," Detective Troy said firmly.

"So you're back to check on the banquet hall?" Dana asked him casually.

"We got a call over the radio about a possible prowler in the area searching out back. Well," he raked his long slender fingers through his thick mousy hair. "I think we know now who that could be." He gave Dana a playfully scolding look.

Dana sighed deeply. She felt heat climb to her cheeks. "Sorry, Troy. I...I was just..."

"I understand you really want to find out who's trying to frame your cousin and ruin the reputation of the café, but again, Dana, please be careful, okay. Leave the grimy work to me and the boys."

"All right, Detective," she said.

He took a piece of wrapper off the lapel of her coat. It probably got stuck on there when she was searching for the notes in the garbage.

"Thanks."

"No problem."

"Um...I'm going to go home and shower and change," she added.

"Good. I'll check on you later. Sorry, I had to cut our date short. We're short-staffed at the station tonight and since I was already at the banquet hall, I volunteered to work on the case."

"Great. So you'll be working late tonight?"

"We're going to the victim's home later."

A light went off in Dana's head. "Troy, shouldn't you do that *sooner* than later?"

Detective Troy arched his brow.

"You mean, you want to be there when we search her apartment?"

HOLIDAY CREAM CUPCAKE & MURDER   61

Dana swallowed hard. "Well, Troy, it's just that....I have a strong suspicion that whoever killed Shags did so because she had some incriminating information on them."

"Now, what makes you think that, Dana?"

"Well, did you find an envelop on Shags?"

"No, it looks as if she..." Detective Troy scratched his head. "You know something. She didn't have her purse on her, did she?"

"Exactly."

"Good observation, Dana."

Dana flushed and smiled bashfully. "It's okay. Women notice certain things."

"Certain things?"

"You know. We look at other women's shoes, their hair and nails and what type of handbag a woman's carrying. I noticed she had a nice little number on her and then it was gone. And there is no way, a woman is going to be caught without her dinner handbag. I mean it has all the essentials. Her makeup for touch ups, her cell phone...I mean everybody needs their cell phone."

"True."

"And it also contains tissues in case one needs it *and* it contains space."

"*Space?*"

"Yes, it contains space, Troy. I hate to tell you this but Shags was collecting some checks at the party."

"Are you sure about this?" Detective Troy whipped out his notepad and pen and began scribbling down some notes.

"I'm very sure about this. I noticed she kept going around to certain guests. I didn't think much of it at the time. But it was something she said to Bea about remembering their discussion. And like Bea, the others looked uncomfortable."

"We already spoke to Bea from the salon."

"Good. Then she probably told you that Shags liked to dig up filthy dirt on everybody she could then use it against them to blackmail them. Now, Bea's purse was half opened and she had an envelop in there."

"Money?" Detective Troy said.

"Possibly. I just couldn't figure out why she carried it to the party. Now, I know she had nothing to do with the murder."

"How do you know that?"

"Because, trust me, I know Bea very well."

"Dana, anyone could be a murderer."

"But not Bea. I just have a hunch. Did you manage to get those photos from Frank?"

"Yes, in fact we did."

"Troy, can I please look at them? Can we go over to Shags' apartment now? It's really important. You said yourself I'm always like a good luck charm on your cases." She gave him a puppy eyed look.

"Dana."

"Troy."

"Very well then. You did manage to find the missing evidence on my last case that the boys missed at that heiress's apartment after her murder. Fine. But please. Do. Not. Touch. Anything."

"I promise. I won't."

HOLIDAY CREAM CUPCAKE & MURDER 63

"HE SAID WHAT?" KATIE said to Dana as they drove off from the Town Hall back to the Victorian.

"Oh, Katie, it was so touching. He told me that garbage couldn't never dampen my beauty."

"Well, he's the one then."

"Katie."

"Seriously, cuz. If you're covered in trash and smell like rotten food and he still thinks you're a princess, he's the one."

Dana playfully rolled her eyes. She then turned the steering wheel to the left as she made a turn on Crom Street toward their home. "I don't know if he's the one, Katie. He was just being nice."

"Wait a minute. Did he wrinkle his nose when he first saw you covered in trash?"

"Well, you were there. Come to think of it, no."

"I didn't see it either. Not from where I was standing. But you know what I did see?"

"What?"

"His eyes. He looked at you as if you were an *adorable* little kitten caught in the trash."

Dana's heart galloped in her chest. She felt warmth creep around her. "Really?" she said softly.

"Really, cuz. Listen, I know you swore you won't get your heart crushed again ...and trust me, I've been there with men, too. I'm divorced, remember?"

"I do, Katie. And I'm so sorry that you're being dragged into this Shags murder investigation, too."

"Yeah, me too. I didn't like her. Even her name reminds me of what she did to my ex-husband. But she didn't deserve to be murdered. Especially over the holidays."

"I know." Dana pulled up to the curb near the Victorian.

"Anyway, don't let that stop you from dating and meeting somebody else, cuz. That's all I'm saying. Look how many times Grandma Rae was married."

"True. She never gave up on finding true love. But she was from a different school of thought, cuz. Besides, her husbands didn't leave her by choice. They all...well, kind of expired."

"I know. But give this guy a chance."

"I don't know, Katie. I really can't handle another broken heart if it doesn't work out. Besides, right now," she said, reaching into her pocket to feel for the torn letters she'd found in the garbage. "We've got to get down to the bottom of Shags' murder!"

Chapter 11

LATER THAT EVENING, after Dana had gone home and showered and changed off into her black leggings and wore her riding leather boots and a knitted long sweater that Grandma Rae had knitted for her a few years ago, Dana was ready to go.

She couldn't wait to shove her dress and stockings into the washer to clean in the heavy cycle after it had been in the garbage.

And speaking of garbage, Katie and Dana had tried to piece together the torn letters she'd found in the garbage bin. It was a letter addressed to the mayor from some guy in Colorado.

Colorado?

Dana wandered why those personal handwritten letters were torn?

She couldn't quite read everything but would go back to them later. She wouldn't bother Detective Troy with any of those details now. She would wait until she could pieced together the letter. It was strange how that letter was handwritten in this day and age of electronic communication. That was rear. But why would the mayor want to get rid of it and why was it addressed to his office, not his home?

"Do you think he had the letter sent to his office because he didn't want his rich wife knowing about his friendship with this guy from Colorado?"

"Possibly." Dana thought about it.

"I think so. Mayor Jones might be mayor of the town, but we all know he's rich because of the wealthy woman he married."

"They'd been married for thirty years."

"I know. And they have no children. So if anything happens to his wife. Her billion dollar inheritance fortune would be all his."

"I'm sure part of his prenup clause was that once he's faithful to his wife—he's good to go if anything happens to her."

"But Shags had been dating him."

"True. That's going to put a kicker in his plans."

"The more I think about it, the more anxious I get. The mayor knows the layout of the Town Hall better than anyone and if Shags did come to collect her paycheck from him—so to speak, then he would have removed her purse, right?"

"Right."

Dana gave herself, one more quick glance in the mirror then brushed her newly shampooed and dried hair.

"I cannot believe you're actually going on a date with a hot cop to a *murder* scene. You guys are strange." Katie grinned at the doorway of Dana's bedroom. Katie had already showered and changed for bed and held a large mug of hot chocolate with whipped cream in her hand. She wore her pink dressing gown that was tied at the waist and her hair was done up into an upsweep.

"Katie, you know that's not exactly what it is," Dana grinned.

"Oh, come on please. You guys have to be the most stubborn and strange couple I've ever met."

HOLIDAY CREAM CUPCAKE & MURDER

"We're not a couple, Katie."

"That's what makes it so strange. I saw the look in both of your eyes. I could feel that electrical chemistry between you two. It was so thick you could cut it with a knife. You both have the hots for each other yet you're trying to avoid the inevitable." Katie grinned and took another sip of her hot steamy chocolate.

Dana could inhale the delicious scent of cinnamon and nutmeg from the mug of hot chocolate. Dana could do with a mug herself and curl up by the fireplace, but not tonight. Tonight, as Katie said, she had a date at the home of a murder victim.

Come to think of it. That *did* sound crazy, didn't it?

"Troy will be here to pick me up soon. Don't wait up."

"Oh, I won't."

Just then Dana felt the furry hairs of her Ginger-haired cat, Truffles, circle around her ankles. "Oh, baby, Mama's going to be out late, so you don't wait up either, okay."

Truffles always managed to warm Dana's heart, even on the coldest of nights, like tonight.

Maybe Katie was right. She had a point. Dana couldn't wait to spend her time with Detective Troy looking for clues at the scene of a crime. Was she weird or what? But her heart leaped in her chest every time she was together with him. Was it because they both loved to solve mystery riddles or in his case, mystery crimes? Was she attracted to him because of his profession or because of him? Did it matter?

Wasn't that the best ingredient for a relationship, as Grandma Rae used to say:

A pinch of love

A dash of honesty
A cup of communication and compatibility.
Patience and understanding

Or something like that, Dana tried hard to remember. But the cup of communication was important. Being able to talk about anything. Dana didn't have much in common with her ex-fiancé. She seemed to have more in common with Detective Troy. They could communicate about solving stuff and he didn't think she was strange like her ex did.

Yeah, Dana and Troy certainly had that cup of communication and compatibility going strong, didn't they?

Grandma Rae always had her own special ingredients for everything, from the cakes she used to bake to the stuff that made up life and everyday living. Gosh, she missed her Grandma Rae like crazy. What would Grandma Rae do in a situation like now? Would she seize the moment? Then again, Grandma Rae had married several times. She believed in love and was never afraid to take chances.

Just then, the sound of the doorbell startled Dana.

"He's here? Already?"

Chapter 12

POLICE CAUTION TAPE surrounded Shags' upscale bachelor apartment that she'd rented on the East side of town. Detective Troy spoke to the cops at the scene and they let him through along with Dana.

She was ever so grateful that he'd allowed her to tag along to help out, especially since she'd discovered clues that his boys had missed at the last investigation.

Dana gaped around the open concept apartment. There was a massive queen sized bed in the far corner. A living room area with a black leather couch and matching leather loveseat, covered in satin red pillows. A red faux fur rug in the center of that living area. Over by the other far corner was a kitchen area and near there was what looked like a make-shift office with a computer desk and a file cabinet along with some files on top of that.

But it also looked as if the place had been ransacked. Things were turned over, drawers were opened. *Somebody* was looking for *something*. Was it incriminating evidence they were looking for? Either way, it looked as if that person had been interrupted and didn't get a chance to finish the job. Half the place looked untouched.

"Hey, what's this?" Dana said noticing some white furry hairs all over the place.

"The landlord said earlier that she has a white-haired cat that sheds like there's no tomorrow."

"Aww. Well, isn't that sweet."

Dana then spotted the furry friend sleeping in her kitty bed looking cozy, oblivious to what was going on. Her heart squeezed in her chest. Did the kitty even know her mommy was…gone? She hoped that somebody kind would be able to take care of the kitty now that Shags was no longer around.

"Did you guys check out the guy that she came in with at the party?"

"He checks out fine. He was just a hired date for the evening. Nothing unusual with him. He wasn't anywhere near Shags when she died."

"So you confirmed with the images from Frank the photographer."

"You do ask a lot of questions, Dana."

She flushed.

"To answer your question. Yes. I checked the images from Frank's camera. The only people near Shags at the time were Katie, Bea, and a few other guests."

"I see." Dana felt her heart plummet in her chest.

Dana also observed there were some boxes scattered around the area. A box by the bed, one by the kitchen and other large packing boxes.

"That's interesting."

"What is?" Detective Troy asked.

"The packing boxes," Dana said walking over to the one by the home office area.

"She just moved here, remember?"

"But that was a few weeks ago."

"Sometimes, it takes people a while to unpack," he said.

"That's true," Dana said, looking closely at the boxes.

"Remember now, don't touch a thing, Dana. If you see anything, just let me know."

"Sure thing, Troy."

Dana's heart was still giddy over what he'd said earlier when he'd found her searching through the trash in the back alley at Town Hall. That was so sweet of him.

Of course, now, she wasn't wearing her black dress that was covered in trash and goodness knew what other liquid waste had been dumped on her. She was freshly showered and shampooed and was all dressed up in her sexy black soft leggings, knee high leather riding boots and her long curve hugging turtle neck jumper that reached her thighs and accentuated her figure. She also donned her other winter coat—she'd already tossed her previous coat into a bag to give to the Berry Cove Dry Cleaners tomorrow when they re-opened.

Troy took his time sifting through some notes on Shags computer desk.

"You know Troy, as a journalist she probably had a file cabinet somewhere with some private paperwork."

"Wouldn't that be on her computer?"

"Not necessarily"

"Not *necessarily*?" Detective Troy arched his brow.

He looked positively gorgeous whenever he did that. She liked the way his chiseled features were highlighted on his face. Strong jawline, beautiful ocean-blue eyes, thick black lashes and shapely eyebrows.

Okay, stop ogling the guy's features, Dana. Focus.

"Dana, storing things on cloud storage and on computers would be the most logical thing for reporters," Detective Troy continued while flipping through some pages in the brown file folder.

"In this day and age of *hacking*?" Dana arched her brow.

Detective Troy melted into a smile. "You *do* have a point, Dana."

Dana tried not to gush. Goodness, she hoped her cheeks weren't turning red—again. "Thanks," she said, quietly.

"What makes you think she keeps a secret file offline?" Detective Troy questioned Dana after moving to another file folder. He probably didn't want to miss anything all the same.

"Well, I know I keep some stuff offline that I wouldn't want anyone else to see. For instance, if she was in fact working on some stories that could be her pay day or nest egg retirement fund, she wouldn't want to risk it being leaked."

"No, she probably wouldn't." He frowned. "You're right, Dana. Sure you don't want to join our special services unit on the force?" He grinned.

"I would um...love to...but...I think I'll hold off for now, thanks. Managing Grandma Rae's café is the sweetest thing I could do right now *and* the safest." A grin curved her lips.

Troy shook his head and smiled. "I don't blame you. To be honest, I rest easier at night knowing that you're working in a safer environment than trying to catch murderers in our homicide division." His voice was low and soft when he said it.

Butterflies fluttered inside Dana's tummy again.

He rests easier at night knowing that I'm working in a safe environment? Oh, my gosh! Is Detective Troy saying that he thinks about me at night? Okay, calm down Dana. He was just saying. That's all.

"Wait a minute."

"What is it?" Detective Troy said as he turned around. He had a brown file folder in his hand from the filing cabinet by the computer.

"The bed."

"What about it?"

Dana got down on her knees and knelt down by the bed. She lifted up the bed skirt. "Troy, there's some sort of clothes storage unit under the bed."

"Yeah, she probably stores her off season clothes in there like a lot of people do."

"I know but...I think that might be a good hiding place to store some documents she didn't want anyone else to see."

Dana pulled out a box filled with envelopes.

Detective Troy went to Dana's side and crouched down. "Let me see that."

As Detective Troy took hold of a large brown envelope and opened it, he sifted through some letters and notes in it.

Dana also looked at another box near the bed. "Troy. I don't think these boxes are from New York."

"What do you mean?"

"It looks as if Shags was planning to buy another place in Berry Cove and upgrade from this fancy bachelor apartment into something more upscale if you know what I mean. "

"Are you sure about that?"

"I'm almost positive. Bea and Inga mentioned that Shags was looking into buying real estate here. Never mind renting."

"Oh, she was, was she?"

"There's one thing about the gossip mill at Bea's Salon is that sometimes there's a little truth in there. A little. And only sometimes, of course."

"Hmm."

"You see a realtor had confirmed that she was looking into some fancy properties."

"I see." Detective Troy sifted through some papers and found some stashes of money and money orders. He frowned.

"What is it?"

"You're right, Dana. There's a lot of what appears to be payout money in here. Looks as if she's been collecting her funds. Maybe she was going to deposit the money soon."

Detective Troy placed all the pages on a table near the living area and spread them out. He then called in the forensic photographer to take a snap shot of the items.

There was a list with names on it and check marks beside some names. Mayor Jones name was also on that list.

Detective Troy pinched his lips together. She could tell he wasn't happy to see that. It looked as if his boss was being blackmailed which would give him a really good motive and the opportunity to see Shags vanish. An envelope with Katie's name on it also lay on the table.

Dana gasped.

Detective Troy opened the envelope. It contained a note.

"Sorry about what happened between us. Hope there's no hard feelings."-Shags M.

Dana's heart melted. "Oh, no. Shags was trying to make amends with Katie. She knew she would be moving here and she's no longer seeing Katie's ex-husband, so she probably figured it would be a good idea to be friends."

Dana felt sadness flood over her.

"It would seem that way," he agreed, "Looks like Shags had some unfinished business she was taking care of."

HOLIDAY CREAM CUPCAKE & MURDER 75

"Well, Troy, Shags had a lot of dirt on a lot of people. Anyone of them could be the killer. But definitely not Katie. That note proves that Katie wouldn't have a motive!"

"But Katie didn't *see* the note yet, Dana." Troy ached his brow.

Dana frowned. "I guess you're right. She didn't see the note."

There was also an envelope with Bea's name on it. It also had some money attached to it.

Was this from a previous payoff?

Then there was the Mayor's envelope. "Colorado. Brandon Jones."

Dana gasped again.

"Dana, what is it? You know something about this, don't you?"

Dana reached into her handbag and pulled out the notes. "Yes, I do. Troy, it looks as if the mayor had some letters addressed to him from Colorado. It was torn up and thrown out in the trash."

Troy frowned. He called one of the uniformed cops to go to the Mayor's home. "Dana, I'm taking you home now. I need to speak with my boss."

"WHAT IS THIS ABOUT, Headly?" Detective Troy interrogated Mayor Jones. The mayor had consistently denied any rumors of seeing Shags earlier in the day.

"I...well, I don't know what to say. That woman was crazy. You know how some tabloid reporters are. Always digging for dirt. I'm a respected politician, Troy and might I remind you, I'm your boss."

Detective Troy tried hard not to back down. But he trusted Dana's instincts—and he trusted his own. His *boss* was hiding something. But what?

Detective Troy paced with his hands in his pockets. Some torn pieces of letters that Dana had found in the garbage were in an evidence bag on the table.

The mayor glanced at the torn letter in the bag.

"That bag was found in your garbage bin at Town Hall." Detective Troy tried to contain himself. If there was one thing he didn't like was someone lying to him point blank. He was willing to risk his job just to prove his point.

"There must be some misunderstanding, Troy."

"Headly, how long have we known each other? Come on. It's me you're talking to."

"Okay, all right." Mayor Jones frowned and walked over by his bar and poured himself some brandy and took a drink. "Can I get you a drink?"

"You know I don't drink on the job, Headly."

"Fine. Good." Mayor Jones finished the contents of the glass and placed it on the counter top. He then wiped his mouth with his hand and sighed deeply.

He walked over by the landing to check that the lights were still off. Probably wanting to make sure that his wife was still asleep.

"Let's go into the study," Mayor Jones said, looking around.

When the two men walked into the study, Mayor Jones closed the sliding French doors shut behind them.

There was a tall seven-foot Christmas Tree by the fireplace that had sparkling lights flashing on it. A star was atop the tree. Detective Troy noticed there were probably hundreds of Christmas cards around the study. Decorating the tree and also strung up on the wall and atop the fireplace mantelpiece. The Jones were certainly very popular. But then again, most wealthy socialites were. And that was what his wife was—a wealthy socialite.

A grand portrait of his wife hung above the fireplace.

"Mrs. Jones looks fabulous in that portrait."

"Yes, she does," Mayor Jones agreed. "She's from a long line of jewelers dating back from the 1750s. The Lyons family. Her maiden name."

"Of course. Yes, I remember reading about her family background." Mrs. Jones had inherited the entire estate from her grandfather worth over billions. That was before she met and married Headly Jones. It had been the wedding of the century then.

"That's why you didn't want her to know about your...affair?" Detective Troy said softly, getting down to the truth.

"Yes," Mayor Jones admitted. "You know how it is, right?"

"No, I don't, sir." Again, Detective Troy's voice was soft and non-judgmental, and as much as he felt sorry for his boss, Troy could never relate to a man cheating on his wife or girlfriend.

Troy was and always had been a one-woman man, that was why he almost lost his mind when his ex-fiancée pulled a number on him and slept with his cousin who happened to be his best friend at the time. It almost killed him. That was why he found it hard to trust another woman. His ex fiancée had been the love of his life at the time—or so he thought. She was supposed to be his best friend and life long partner in everything. How could he trust a woman again?

Still, that was history now. He needed to focus on the murder investigation at hand.

"Well," Mayor Jones said, pretending to fix something on the Christmas Tree, avoiding Troy's gaze. "My wife comes from a long line of successful jewelers. Many thought I married her for her money, but I did not. Well, okay, maybe that was a plus, but I do love her. I really do. And it works both ways. She never really had to work in her life either. So she was happy to be a politician's wife, instead of just the daughter and granddaughter of a magnate."

"Okay."

"Well," Mayor Jones sighed deeply as he continued. "We started having trouble in the marriage decades ago when we first married when she found out she couldn't...have any children."

"I'm sorry to hear that. But you've been married now thirty years, is that correct?"

"About that. But don't tell Mrs. Jones, I forgot the year we got married."

Detective Troy resisted the urge to grin. "I won't."

"Anyway, I'd met Shags back in New York and we...well, we had a moment of indiscretion. It was the first time I had ever cheated on my wife, I swear. I had never done it before. But that was in New York. I'd never even been to her place in Berry Cove. I stopped seeing her back then."

"And you wouldn't want your wife to find out about the affair because of the prenup agreement, right?"

HOLIDAY CREAM CUPCAKE & MURDER

The mayor turned to Detective Troy stunned. "What? How did you hear about that?"

"Seems like Shags already had the information on you, Mayor. She was blackmailing you, wasn't she?"

The mayor turned his head away and looked out at the multi-paned window where the snow flakes fell heavy outside. "She tried to."

"Is that why you killed her, Mayor?"

"What? No. I swear to you, I did not kill Shags! Why would I?"

"Because she threatened to destroy your marriage and your retirement nest egg, sir. She had too much information on you. And including that letter. I pieced it together. It wasn't the first time you had cheated on your wife, sir. You cheated on her about twenty-three years ago, didn't you?"

The mayor swallowed hard. He looked down. "Yes. I...I did. You're right."

"Why did you lie to me, Headly?"

"I..." He clasped his hands together. "She would kill me if she found out I had a son."

Detective Troy's eyes opened wide. So it was true then. If Dana hadn't showed him those pieces of paper from the garbage bin, letters from the mayor to his son asking him to come and stay with him in Berry Cove so that he could get to know him better, Troy would never had known. He really owed Dana a lot for this. A lot.

"You see, I travel quite a lot, visiting other mayors in other cities. And well, I met this nice waitress back in Colorado on one of my trips and the last thing I know, we had an affair. Then she told me about my son years later."

"So you only found out about him recently?"

"Yes, that's right. I found out about him very recently."

"And so did Shags."

"Yes. That's why I hated that witchy woman. Okay, I admit it. She had no right meddling in my personal affairs. She had been blackmailing me into keeping quiet about my affair with her. Then she somehow intercepted my calls and found out about my past dealings with Becky, my son Julian's mother."

Detective Troy sighed and wiped his brow. "Okay, so let me get this straight. She decided to up the price and charge more for her silence when she found out the living proof that you'd been unfaithful to your wife?"

"Yes, she wanted five million dollars. How on earth would I take that out of my wife's account without her knowing it? Then Shags told me to buy an expensive property and pretend it's an investment but put it in her name. In Shags' name. That woman was crazy, she was. But I did *not* kill her. I'm not going to lie to you, I thought about it, fantasized about it. But I didn't do it, Troy. You have to believe me."

"It's hard to believe you, boss when you keep lying to me like a bad habit."

"But I'm telling the truth now."

"You didn't go to her home and threaten her—or go through her things?"

"No. I've never *been* to Shags' apartment. I swear to you."

"All right. Where is your son now?"

"I'd rather not say. I don't want him to be involved in this."

Detective Troy ran his fingers through his hair. "Headly, this is a murder investigation, sir. No need to tell you the seriousness of this case."

"All right. All right, but please, I don't want the media to get wind of this. I really don't want my wife to find out. Not this way. I'll have to break it to her gently."

"I'm listening."

"His name is Julian and I got him a job catering the Christmas party as a waiter."

Detective Troy froze.

"As a waiter?"

"Yes, I wanted to get to know him better. He had dropped out of college and was living with some friends in a run down place back in Colorado. I paid his air fare and offered to take care of him here."

Detective Troy wrote down some more notes and combed his hair again with his fingers, a nervous habit he had to learn to get rid of. But right now, he couldn't believe how this night was unfolding.

"Sir, I'm going to ask you to surrender your passport and make no plans to leave town. You know the procedure."

"Yes, I know. But where would I go now anyway?"

"I don't know. But just make sure that I can find you. I'll be back."

Detective Troy had interviewed a few waiters after Shags was found murdered at the party but now he had to go back and speak to Julian.

Chapter 13

"WELL, DANA, YOU WERE right," Detective Troy said the next morning to Dana. They both had a quiet booth at the Breakfast Place on the other side of town. Christmas songs sounded through the speakers while patrons ate their meals. The waiters were so cheerful and each wore red Santa hats as they took orders.

It seemed like most businesses were in the spirit of the holiday season. The baristas at the Cozy Cupcakes Café also donned Santa hats and matching red aprons. They also had the satellite radio set to a station playing round the clock Christmas songs—but of course the holiday spirit had been slightly dampened with the false rumors circulating around town that one of the famous Cozy Cupcakes Café's Holiday Cream Cupcakes had been poisoned and had killed the town's infamous new tabloid gossip columnist. That rumor never mentioned that the victim had what appeared to be a small stab wound in the back.

Right now the tune playing over the speakers was *Deck the Halls with Boughs of Holly*. Well, Dana sure felt as if *she'd* been decked in the halls of holly after those killer cupcakes rumors hit the town.

Troy had asked Dana to meet him at the Breakfast Place so that they could have a quiet conversation. Meeting her at the Cozy Cupcakes Café wouldn't have been such a good idea. Not

HOLIDAY CREAM CUPCAKE & MURDER

with the holiday season in full swing and many busy customers asking about Shags' murder.

"I was right?" Dana echoed.

"Yes," Detective Troy said, adding a pinch of sugar to his steaming mug of black coffee. "Seems like Shags was blackmailing the mayor big time."

"Oh, dear. I'm really sorry to hear that. But I knew there was something dodgy about those torn letters in the garbage bin. Do you think he...um...he did it?" Dana tried to keep her voice low even though the holiday music played over the speakers.

"I can't say right now, but he really has a strong motive. Not to mention telling the truth is a bit hard for him."

"You know, I found him near the utility box that night, too."

"You did? Why didn't you say anything before?"

"It skipped my mind. But I really think there's more to the story than what he's feeding us, Troy. I don't know why, but I just feel that way. Something is bothering me."

"What is it?"

"I can't quite put my finger on it. This is a crazy riddle. The missing clue is right there and I can see it, but I *can't* see it."

"You make no sense."

"Let me explain. Something just doesn't fit to this story, but I don't know what it is. The mayor must have been looking to cover his tracks. He probably went to Shags' apartment to search through any evidence she might have against him."

"No. He swore to me that he's never been there." Detective Troy took out some photos that were taken by Frank the

Gazette photographer. "Do you recognize anyone in any of these photographs, Dana?"

Dana pushed her plate of scrambled eggs and half-eaten pancakes aside and sifted through the photos on the table. "Hmm. Not really. Oh, he's really cute. I remember the waiter asking us if we wanted a cupcake."

"This one?" Troy pointed to the photo to confirm.

"Yes, why?"

"Well, that's Julian. The mayor confirmed that's his son. They'd *only just met* recently and he got him a job at the catering department for the town."

"Really?" Dana looked again. "Well, that's very strange. Do you think he would have something to do with it?"

"Not likely. What motive would he have?"

"True. But then there was something that I found odd," Dana said, taking another mouthful of the buttered pancakes and syrup.

"What is it?"

"The mayor's secretary, Sarah. She's a contract employee. Looks like Shags had a file on her, too. I noticed a file marked Sarah. It must be her."

"She did have a file on her, on everyone in the town practically. But that doesn't mean anything. Sarah has cooperated with the investigation so far."

Just then Troy's cell phone rang and he pulled it out of his breast jacket to answer it. While he was speaking on the phone, Dana went through more photos.

"Well, Dana, looks like the cupcake that was intended for Shags had been laced with cyanide poisoning."

Dana gasped. Well that ruined her appetite. Her heart pounded in her chest. Her stomach fell. "I can't believe someone would poison one of my cupcakes—again. Trying to frame my café."

"Well, it was done at the party. There was a syringe that was found. No fingerprints on it. But she'd also been stabbed in the back with a syringe with a long needle. That was how she died. I just spoke with the lab."

"Oh, that's awful. So whoever did it planned to poison her with my cupcake and when she'd refused to eat it, they went to plan B and injected her with the poison but left the cupcake at the scene to make it look as if she'd eaten it?"

"Looks that way, unfortunately."

"But who would do that? How? Why?"

"I'm going to find out one way or the other, Dana. And I'm going to be having another word with the mayor soon." Troy narrowed his eyes. He barely touched his own breakfast. He'd ordered a large breakfast for the two of them but he clearly wasn't in the mood for feasting.

And right now, neither was Dana.

Chapter 14

"SO LET ME GET THIS straight," Katie said later that evening, while adding candy canes as the finishing touches to the Christmas tree at the Victorian. The tree looked gorgeous with the glowing gold light bulbs and the shiny golden Christmas balls. "You don't think the mayor did it?"

They had procrastinated decorating at the home for sometime now. They'd been busy decorating the Cozy Cupcakes Café instead.

Dana had just finished baking Grandma Rae's famous lasagna with bubbling mozzarella cheese and a secret blend of seasoning. She'd cut a few slices and served on plates.

"Well, I didn't quite say that. I think he probably could have done it." Dana placed a glass of creamy eggnog with nutmeg and cinnamon at each setting on the table.

Truffles purred gently by the fireplace in the grand living room near to the open dining room area. She had already had her dinner and was settled in her usual spot.

"Well, what are you saying then?" Katie came down from the stool after she was finished with the Christmas tree.

"I'm saying that there is more to the picture. Troy said that the mayor had never been to Shags apartment. So he wasn't the one who had ransacked it. But somebody was looking for something. I need to find out who?"

"Who do you think it could be?"

"Well, what if his wife found out about the affair and about...his secret son?"

"That's true." Katie made her way to the dinner table after she washed her hands in the kitchen sink.

The two ladies sat down. "Thank you Lord for blessing this food and for providing for us, Amen." Dana opened her eyes after her grace.

"Well, that was brief."

"You know Grandma Rae used to always have those long-winded graces where she asks the Lord to bless the hands that prepared the food, the people in the world who didn't have any to eat..."

"And to count our blessings and..."

"To remember the war vets and the pets..."

"And a hundred different causes."

"You know, bless her heart, she was really sweet. Always thinking about others..."

"Yeah, true, cuz. But we'd be starving by the time she was done with her one hour grace."

"Exactly, and after a long day at the café. I'm starved." Both ladies laughed. "Well, it's always good to be grateful for everything."

"It is. And I'm so grateful that the cops are easing off me, too," Katie said, "They said they won't need me for further questioning at this time."

"They did? When were you going to tell me this?" Dana dug into her slice of lasagna.

"Oh, one of the detectives spoke to me at the café while you were in the back with the suppliers. He just dropped by briefly.

"Well, that's good news, cuz."

"Thanks for your help with the investigation. If it hadn't been for those torn letters you'd found in the garbage can, I might have still been the lead suspect."

"Well, I know you had nothing to do with it, cuz. Besides, there are others with a stronger motive. Shags might have hurt you in the past, but you were not on her radar to blackmail."

"True. What about Bea? You mentioned that Bea had a secret that Shags knew about?"

"Yes, and I spoke with Bea earlier. She told me that she wanted to hide the fact that...well, she told me not to tell anyone."

"Dana!"

"Katie!"

"Come on, cuz. You can't hold back on me."

"Katie, you know I love you cuz, but I promised I would keep her secret. Besides, what does it matter? She told me that she had nothing to do with the murder."

"So who else does that leave?"

"Mayor Jones *and* his wife." Dana dropped her fork on the table.

"What is it, cuz?"

"What about Frank, the photographer? I saw an envelope with his name on it in Shags' apartment. I think she'd been trying to get some dirt on him, too."

"Why would she do that?"

"I don't know but tomorrow morning, I'm going to find out. He was snapping away with his camera. He knew where everyone was at the time of the blackout. He was in a good position to know."

"Yes, he was, wasn't he?"

Chapter 15

"YES, I HATED HER. BUT I didn't killer her," Frank told Dana as they walked in the Town Square the next morning.

"Thanks for meeting with me, Frank. I just had to know if you'd seen anything suspicious on the night of Shags' murder. Everyone still believes that Katie poisoned one of our Holiday Cream Cupcakes to get back at Shags which is simply a lie!"

"I know. I don't for one thing believe a word about the killer cupcakes rumor."

Dana felt her heart squeeze at the sound of the words Killer Cupcakes. Grandma Rae would have had a coronary if she were alive and hearing that about her beloved creamy cupcakes—the ones she labored over with love in her heart. She'd always believe in baking with love and doing everything with love. It was her motto, her life, her way of living. Dana knew she had to quiet these rumors once and for all and find the real cold-blooded killer at large.

Speaking of cold, the morning brought some chill with the temperature dropping. Snow flakes fell softly but it was cold that morning.

"I guess it's no secret now. I was up for editor of the newspaper."

"You were? Congratulations!"

"Not so fast. When Shags blew into town on her broom, things changed fast. We never agreed on things creatively. I'm

HOLIDAY CREAM CUPCAKE & MURDER   91

a photographer but I also have ten years of experience editing a newspaper back in Colorado."

Dana's heart stopped. "In *Colorado*?"

"Yeah. But I was caught up in some trouble back then."

"Oh, what kind of trouble?"

"Let's just say that I got into some gambling debts and into some trouble with the law with drugs. Not something I'm proud of."

"Oh, no. Sorry to hear that. So Shags caught wind of that and she was going to use it against you."

"Bingo. I pulled out my application for Chief Editor. I knew she wanted the position. Heck, she wanted to take over the Gazette. I heard she was coming up with the money to rescue it from possible bankruptcy and persuaded the board to see her creative vision of competing with online tabloids." Frank rolled his eyes. "I knew it was a mistake. It was all a big mistake. Anyway, I didn't kill her."

"I believe you, Frank," Dana said. "For some reason. I do believe you're telling the truth."

Dana stopped outside the Berry Cove Cleaners to pick up her dry cleaning. She badly needed her puffy winter coat. The one she was wearing now was not warm enough for the drop in temperature.

"You picking up some clothes?" Frank commented as he stopped outside the drycleaners with her.

"Actually, my winter coat. I...had a little accident with it." When she'd fallen into the dumpster and had trash poured over her at the Town Hall, but she wasn't about to divulge that information to Frank.

"See you later, Frank."

"See you. Let me know if you need anything else."

"I will."

"Good morning, Dana. Your coat's ready." Dillan picked up a clear plastic bag with Dana's winter coat and hung it up on the rack beside her so she could see it.

"Great. Thanks so much. How much do I owe you?"

"Five dollars."

"Only that?"

"You know your Grandma Rae was a fabulous woman, Dana. She really helped me out in the early days. I told her that she would have a discount for life. You're her family so it applies to you, too."

"Aww, you are so sweet."

"Thanks, Dana. No pun intended but so are you."

She grinned and gave him the cash and picked up her jacket.

The door chimed sounded as someone came in behind Dana.

"Oh, Lilly," Dillan said to the customer. "I have the mayor's suit here."

Dana turned around. It was another secretary who worked for the mayor.

"Thanks," Lilly said to Dillan. "Hope you got all those white cat hairs out. It really ruined his black suit."

"It wasn't easy, I had no idea the mayor owned a cat."

Lilly paid the price for the suit and ignored Dillan's comment. "Well, have a good day."

"You, too."

"Dillan," Dana said after Lilly left. "What was that about?"

Dana felt her heart palpitate in her chest.

"Oh, nothing. Typical politician who needs things to be done right away. We told him it would take a couple days since the suit is delicate and the cat hairs are numerous. His wife usually brings in his suits, but I guess she's busy and the secretary is doing it."

"He lied about being in the apartment!" Dana said, almost to herself. Those cat hairs were probably from Shags' apartment. The mayor didn't *have* any cats!

"Sorry, what was that?"

"Oh, nothing Dillan." Dana grabbed her coat and ran out of the store. Her heart pounding a mile a minute. She had to speak with Troy fast!

"Yes, Dana." Troy sounded distracted on the phone while working at his office. Dana was glad to reach him on her cell.

She told him about her dealings at the Berry Cove Cleaners.

Dana was now at Gary's Garage, next door to the cleaners.

"It's all right, Dana. The mayor confessed to me later that he'd been at Shags' apartment."

Her heart sank. "But why didn't he tell you this before?"

"He said he was nervous about his wife finding out about their affair but he apparently came clean with her and now he's telling us everything."

"You mean he's trying really hard to cover his tracks."

"Dana. I think we need to let it go, all right?"

Dana felt deflated. She waited at the garage while Gary the mechanic worked on her car.

"Okay, fine." Dana ended her call with Troy who seemed as if he had better things to do right now than to entertain her suspicions. But there was something really odd about the mayor's behavior. He wasn't telling everything. He was covering up something or—for someone!

Maybe Katie was right. Maybe Dana did have an overactive imagination. Maybe she really did need some sleep. Maybe there really wasn't much to the investigation as she was making to be.

She sighed deeply. She glanced at her watch. She'd better get going soon. She was expecting another shipment of Christmas Holiday cupcake wrappers at the café later.

"Well, that's about it," Gary said as he wiped his hands on a blue cloth. "The car looks good. Always remember to get a tune up regularly, Dana."

"I will. You know how busy it gets sometimes."

"True."

Dana felt her heart stop when she glanced over at a white car that was hoisted up in the far corner. It had a dent on it with some grey paint.

"Everything all right, Dana?" Gary asked looking puzzled.

Dana kept looking at the car and thought she recognized the plates!

It had to be the mayor's. There were too many clues pointing to his guilt. And she was not going to let this one slip away so fast.

Chapter 16

DANA FELT QUEASY IN her stomach. "Ever had a moment where you're looking at something? Like the answer is right *there* in front of you, but you can't quite pin it?" she said to Katie.

"Sure. Happens all the time, why? What are you looking at, cuz?"

Dana tapped her pencil on her chin as she glanced at the article on the screen.

"Oh, that's the story about the power outage, right? What about it, cuz?"

"Katie, the mayor had a large dent in the front of his white car that had been fixed recently. I saw it hoisted up at Gary's Garage when I went to have my car serviced."

"So?"

"Well, Troy mentioned that the mayor left him in his office for a while as he attended to a private call in another room. What if it wasn't a private call?"

"But Dana that makes no sense. What are you getting at? Why would the mayor *stage* something like that?"

The article was sitting there on the screen, tormenting the cookies out of Dana. There was something very odd about it.

Truffles climbed onto her lap as usual. "Hey, sweetie. Mommy's just trying to figure something out here. Wish I knew what I was looking..."

Dana's eyes opened wide.

She re-read the old news story once again dated more than a year ago.

BERRY COVE GAZETTE:

Outage reduced power to 852 homes and businesses in the area.

Berry Cove Fire Department confirms a pick-up truck hit a utility box at Brock Street and Maple Avenue. Photos from the scene shows there was a fire after the crash. No word on injuries.

Dana's heart leaped in her chest when she continued to read the story. Something struck a chord inside her.

More than 900 homes and businesses were without power Friday evening Berry Cove Utilities reported.

"More than 900 homes and businesses in the area were without power that evening," Dana said, almost to herself.

Dana looked carefully at the map beside the article of the area where the outage occurred and she studied the distance from the utility box to the Town Hall.

Hmm.

"So what? Dana, stuff like that happens all the time," Katie added, puzzled. "What's the big deal?"

"That's just it, Katie. Sometimes we never suspect the obvious. What a *coincidence* and a *convenience* for the killer that there was an outage at the Town Hall during the Christmas party. And I think I know *how* they did it."

"Dana, you can't be serious. I know you have a knack of coming up with the most unusual tales for your mystery riddles blog, but this is a bit far fetch, don't you think? Not to mention implausible. Do you really think the killer rammed his truck into the utility box down the street knowing it would knock out power to..." Katie froze.

HOLIDAY CREAM CUPCAKE & MURDER

"Doesn't sound so implausible now, does it?"

"But Dana, that's crazy. It would take a good ten minutes to walk from the utility box to the hall to kill Shags then return to the scene. Not to mention, why would he risk killing himself by causing a fire or explosion or electrical shock? Think about it, Sherlock, you ram your vehicle into a utility box, you're asking for serious trouble—you're asking to meet your maker."

Dana frowned. Katie *did* have a point. But something was missing. Something huge. It was staring her in the face but she still couldn't see it.

She mulled over the rest of the article.

According to the utility's website, 1,126 customers lost power at 6.25 p.m. Friday afternoon. The utility said it was aware of the outage and worked to restore power.

The outage was centered in the area northeast of the corner Brock Street and Maple Avenue and Riverside Drive.

"We've heard reports that a car crashed into a utility box and caused a transformer to explode," a witness reported hearing an explosion in the area.

Just then a eureka struck Dana.

"What it is, cuz?" Katie said noticing the expression on Dana's face.

"What did you just say?" Dana turned to Katie, her face lit up.

"I said, what it is, cuz?"

"No. Before that."

Katie shrugged. "I don't know, you ram your vehicle into a utility box, you're asking for serious trouble?"

"No, no, after that."

"You're asking to meet your maker."

Truffles purred with delight.

"Bingo." Dana flipped the screen to another web page on her MacBook.

"Okay, cuz, you've got me a bit worried now."

"No worries, Katie. I think I've found Shag's killer."

Dana mulled over the information she'd found earlier and was able to put two and two together. Hopefully, two and two would equal four in this case. She really needed to get hold of Troy very quickly.

Dana then searched online for a website in Colorado.

Colorado. She tapped into some more information about anything she could find on Mayor Jones and his visit to Colorado.

Dana then whipped out her cell phone and dialed Troy's cell.

"I do hope you're going to have Troy and the boys in blue go down to see the killer," Katie said, taking a sip of her hot chocolate in her holiday mug with the Santa Clause on it.

"Oh, no cuz. If there's one thing I learned it's that people are not going to open up to the cops so easily. Troy knows that, too. Of course, he's concerned about my safety. He always tries to convince me to let his men handle it, but whenever I explain the situation to him, he agrees. And whenever I do go to speak to a person of interest, Troy's near by to back me up."

"Isn't that a risk, Dana?"

"It is, but lives are at stake here, Katie. Including your freedom. We don't want to risk letting the culprit slip away."

"Of course not," Katie agreed.

Chapter 17

"ARE YOU SURE ABOUT this, Dana?" Detective Troy said, a concerned look in his eyes. She sat in his office after she'd told him her theory.

"I'm very sure, Troy. We don't' have much time. You need to get your boys down there at the garage to confirm my suspicions."

"We can't just go waltzing in and asking for client's information, Dana. Not without a warrant. There are privacy laws."

"I know, Troy. But that's what the real killer is counting on."

"Dana, do you know what you're saying?"

She swallowed hard. She was really getting in over her head, now wasn't she? But her hunch was very strong here. She needed to clear her cousin's name and the reputation of the Cozy Cupcakes Café. Her Grandma's legacy and business would go down to crumbs if word gets out they were tied to Shags' murder. Not to mention a cold-blooded killer would be loose as a goose.

"You're asking me to investigate my boss?" Detective Troy asked incredulously.

"I...um...I never thought about it like that, Troy. I...I guess you're right."

"I work for the mayor of this town, Dana. It's not that easy to point sticky fingers at the big man, not without some sort of strong evidence."

She sighed heavily.

"But, I'll tell you what. I've got a car at the garage. I'll ask some questions. That's all."

"And hopefully, they'll be able to confirm my suspicions," she said.

"Are you sure about what you thought you saw?"

"Troy, I've never been more sure. There's definitely a change in color at the front of the vehicle. He recently had some paint work done."

Troy frowned. "Good observation, Dana. I will check it out."

If there's one thing Dana knew it was that Troy didn't stand for corruption in any office. He loathed anyone who abused their power in office. Anyone.

Dana admired his nobility and the fact that he would put his neck on the line to do the right thing.

"Thanks, Troy. Remember those torn letters I found in the garbage."

He pinched his lips together. "Which were obtained in the wrong way," he reminded her.

"Hey, I just happened to glance in the garbage. If there wasn't a power cut at the time and if it didn't take time for the machine to reset, he would have shredded the evidence of those letters from his son, the waiter."

"So you think Shags found out about the son and was blackmailing him, threatening to tell his wife about the illegitimate son he had on the side?" Troy arched his brow.

"Something like that. But not quite."

"Dana."

"Troy."

"Yes, sir," a uniformed officer stepped into Troy's office.

"I'm going to need you to check something out for me, Pete."

"Sure thing, boss."

"Dana," Troy turned to Dana after Pete left, "I really hope you're right about this."

She swallowed hard. "So do I."

Chapter 18

"THE MAYOR WILL BE WITH your shortly, Miss Sweet," Sarah, his secretary said as she finished typing up a memo. She'd just buzzed Mayor Jones from the reception area.

"Working so hard during the holiday season?" Dana tried to make small talk and sound as casual as possible as she glanced around at the wondrous holiday decorations. There was a large red Christmas Poinsettia plant sitting on the top of the reception desk where Sarah sat. A tall Christmas tree with gold-colored shimmering lights decorated with many gifts underneath. And a tray of holiday cupcakes from the Cozy Cupcakes Café.

Dana swallowed hard. Her heart galloped in her chest.

"You know, the office is always busy all year round," Sarah replied with a warm smile.

"Of course."

Just then Dana's cell phone rang which caused her to jolt. She glanced at the screen.

Troy Anders.

Her heart leaped in her chest. Why on earth did she always react that way whenever she saw his name? She drew in a deep breath and answered it quietly. "Hey," she said casually.

"Hey, yourself, Dana. You were right."

"I was?"

"Dana, be very careful. I have my men there, okay."

She nodded. "Okay, thanks, Troy."

Okay, here goes.

"Is the mayor ready yet?" Dana said, getting up from her seat in the waiting area and approaching the large oak reception desk.

"Not yet."

Dana's voice was soothing and calm. "It must have been really hard for the mayor's wife to have discovered he had a son on the side. They'd been married thirty years, right?"

Sarah looked uncomfortable as she glanced up from her computer screen. "What was that?"

"I'm just saying, the mayor and his wife had been married for 30 years. And Shags must have found out that he had a 23-year-old son in Colorado."

Sarah looked a bit nervous. "I...um...I guess. Are y-you saying that's why he killed Shags? To keep her quiet from not telling his wife?"

"It would make a very good case," Dana agreed. "I thought so myself, too. But then I looked into all *other* possibilities."

"What do you mean?"

"I thought of who could possibly want Shags dead."

"The mayor, right?"

"Wrong. It was *you*, Sarah. *You* had the most to lose."

"What?" Sarah sprang to her feet. "Are you crazy? What are you talking about? Why would *I* want Shags dead?"

"Because she knew your little scheme, Sarah. It's over," Dana said calmly with sadness in her tone. "It's very sad what you did out of desperation and fear."

"You're crazy, you are. I'm calling security."

"I don't think that would be necessary."

Sarah froze.

"You see, I thought it was odd at first when you left to get some ice at the Christmas party. That was my first clue."

"Because I had to get *ice*? Stupid girl. I don't know what you're talking about."

"You said you had to get some ice and left the party while guests were coming in. That was after Shags had arrived."

"So what? I wasn't there, was I? I came back *after* she...was killed."

"Yes, you did. That's what puzzled me. Anyway, I had tripped over Shags' body and hurt my ankle. I went to the freezer to grab an ice pack and was *stunned* to see how the freezer was already overstuffed with ice. Then it clicked later. You had said you were out of ice. But there was plenty in the freezer. Tons."

Sarah folded her arms across her chest and pinched her lips tight. Her eyes narrowed on Dana. "So...I...made a mistake. I thought we were out of ice."

"No you didn't Sarah, you needed an *excuse* to leave the party to run your vehicle into the utility box knowing full well that it would knock out power to the area—because someone had accidentally done that last year. It was a big thing here at the Town Hall—that's when everyone knew that the utility box on Brock and Maple controls the power in the area."

Sarah's eyes narrowed. "Did you check the mayor's car? Maybe he had something to with it."

"That's what I thought, too. His car *was* involved in that incident. It's been confirmed now. But *he* wasn't the one driving it. As his assistant, you had access to his vehicle. You run errands for him all the time, remember? Both you and his other secretary, Lilly."

HOLIDAY CREAM CUPCAKE & MURDER 105

"Clever. But why would I want Shags dead? I don't have a *motive*, silly girl."

"Oh, but you do. Shags used to have everybody under her little surveillance including everyone working for the mayor's office. You knew that he had a son because you open his mail and send his mail on his behalf."

Sarah got up and paced nervously. "So what?"

"You had a pay day coming as they would say. You're in over your head in debt, especially gambling debt. You needed money fast. The mayor and his wife are beyond rich. They're worth over a billion. He had a son in Colorado and had been sending money to him, but his son wanted nothing to do with him."

"So?"

"You contacted his son on the mayor's behalf and that's when you found your opportunity. His real son had recently died in a car accident. The son's roommate didn't know his pal had a rich daddy back in Berry Cove. Instead of reporting back to the mayor of his son's death, you schemed with his son's *roommate* to *impersonate* his son in order to claim the inheritance and you would split the money. Since the mayor *never met* his real son he wouldn't know the difference. The two men had similar physical traits—and the mother of the mayor's son died years ago. It was the perfect scheme, wasn't it?"

"Ha! That's preposterous."

"Is it?"

"His fake son managed to wiggle his way into the mayor's real son's effects since he had access as a roommate to all the letters that had been sent to the real son. And he somehow managed to convince the mayor to get him a job as a waiter.

That's how you did it. You couldn't have gotten back here in time to stab Shags with the poisonous syringe. So his fake son did it while the power was cut. You knew Shags had threatened to expose you and your little scam to the mayor—and to the police. By the way, the mayor's son Julian—or the imposter named Julian-whose real name is Carter—already ratted you out. So you may as well come clean," Dana lied in her last sentence.

Sarah swallowed hard. She looked as if she was about to have a full blown panic attack.

"All right. I went along with it. But it was Carter's idea. He needed the money more than I did. We started dating, long distance. I thought we could be together. He seemed like a nice guy."

"A nice guy who was a *con*?" Dana arched a brow. "And it was working well for a while, wasn't it?"

"Yes, it was. Until that nosey little witchy woman, Shags, moved to town. It was none of her business. We weren't planning on hurting anyone. We just needed to make some fast dough, that's all. The Jones are loaded with cash. They wouldn't miss a thing. It's not like they would even notice a million dollars gone from their account. They have billions!"

Dana shook her head, feeling sorry for Sarah. Sorry that she felt that murder was the only way out. "Sarah, that's an awful way to want money. You would be hurting them either way."

Just then Detective Troy came in with his men. "Thanks, Dana."

Dana sighed deeply and nodded with sadness.

"Sarah Mayton, I'm placing you under arrest for suspicion of murder and accessory before the fact. You have the right to remain silent..." Detective Troy read Sarah her rights.

Why on earth didn't Dana feel any better? Katie's name was cleared and the Cozy Cupcakes Café was in the clear where their *killer* cupcakes were concerned.

But something was missing.

Chapter 19

"HOW COULD YOU THINK something is missing? Those scam artists are going to be locked away for good."

"I know," Dana said quietly, topping the tray of Holiday Cream cupcakes with little mistletoes.

A large beautiful Christmas Mistletoe hung from the door frame of the café. The café was closed for another twenty minutes until the Christmas crowd came in. It was going to be busy today as it was Christmas Eve.

Inga and the rest of the team were out back getting things ready. The scent of vanilla, nutmeg and cinnamon permeated the air. The fire crackled in the large stone fireplace in the café's dining area.

It was certainly cozy in there, but it just didn't feel the same in Dana's heart for some reason. Not yet.

Maybe she would feel different tomorrow. Grandma Rae used to love the holidays and she missed her like crazy.

"That's what's missing," Dana said, almost to herself as she put the finishing touches to the Holiday Cream Cupcakes display.

"What's missing?"

"Christmas is about love. Grandma Rae used to always say it was hard on those who were lonely. And for the first time, cuz. I feel..." Dana sighed deeply. "Alone."

"I never thought about it like that."

Even Katie was dating one of the supply delivery guys. He was a cute guy who was finishing up college and working in his family's business part time.

Dana felt so happy for her cousin, Katie deserved happiness. She wished she hadn't been so distant with Troy, he was probably trying to get close to her as Katie had observed, but Dana kept pushing him away emotionally.

Then there was Sarah the secretary who, even though her choice was all wrong, fell in love with that Carter scam artist guy. But she thought he was a nice guy—didn't know he was a murderer.

"Grandma Rae used to always say there was magic in mistletoes. I don't know if I believe it."

"You should, cuz. I believe in the magic of the Christmas spirit. And the season of giving...and forgiving as Grandma Rae would say."

"True. I'm so glad we're all going to give Shags a nice memorial next weekend. I think it would be fitting and a way to move forward. We have to look at her good points, not her...well, her mischievous points."

"That was Grandma Rae's way, I guess."

"It sure was..." Dana gasped.

A shadow moved near the café outside the window. It was early in the morning and still very dark and frosty outside.

"What it is? Should we call the police?" Katie asked.

Dana grinned. "I think *that* won't be necessary." Her heart leaped in her chest. She quickly opened the door lock and the chime sounded.

Troy had come in with a large red gift box in his hand. "I almost forgot to give you something."

"Oh, Troy. That's so sweet of you," Dana gushed.

"That's not all I forgot to do, Dana. Our date that night at the Mayor's party had been interrupted, remember?" His voice was soft and smooth.

Her heartbeat leaped in her throat.

"Y-yes, I remember," she whispered.

Detective Troy glanced up at the mistletoe hanging above them with a grin. He then inched closer to her. She could inhale the sweet scent of his aftershave. His scent was sweetly intoxicating.

He then brushed his lips gently against hers and kissed her in a way she'd never been kissed before. He held her around her waist and she melted into his warmth.

Whatever was missing, she had finally found.

If that wasn't the holiday magic Grandma Rae spoke about, she didn't know what was.

THANK YOU FOR READING *A Dana Sweet Cozy Mystery*. For a limited time only, you can claim a FREE copy of the bonus short story, *Strawberry Meringue Cupcake & Murder (Book 3.5)* here: https://www.instafreebie.com/free/2OZGw

---

DANA SWEET COZY MYSTERY series:
Strawberry Cream Cupcake & Murder (Book 1)
Blueberry Cream Cupcake & Murder (Book 2)
Chocolate Cream Cupcake & Murder (Book 3)
Strawberry Meringue Cupcake & Murder (Book 3.5)

Vanilla Cream Cupcake & Murder (Book 4)
Holiday Cream Cupcake & Murder (Book 5)
Valentine's Cream Cupcake & Murder (Book 6)
Buttercream Cupcake & Murder (Book 7)

Coming soon...

More delightful stories set in the cozy small town of Berry Cove in the Dana Sweet Cozy Mystery series.

ABOUT THE AUTHOR:

Ann S. Marie enjoys reading and writing cozy mysteries and solving mind-boggling puzzles with intriguing suspects. Join her email list for updates on more cozy mysteries that will make your toes curl and your heart smile. You can send her an email at annsmarie.author@gmail.com with the subject line: **Email Sign-Up**.

She loves to hear from readers.

You can also like her Facebook page: www.Facebook.com/annsmariebooks[1]

http://annsmarieauthor.blogspot.com

---

1. http://www.Facebook.com/annsmariebooks

Printed in the USA
CPSIA information can be obtained
at www.ICGtesting.com
LVHW052143030823
754323LV00033B/636